EMPEROR
OF THE AIR
◆ ◆ ◆

OTHER HOUGHTON MIFFLIN
LITERARY FELLOWSHIP AWARDS

E. P. O'Donnell, *Green Margins*

Dorothy Baker, *Young Man with a Horn*

Robert Penn Warren, *Night Rider*

Joseph Wechsberg, *Looking for a Bluebird*

Ann Petry, *The Street*

Elizabeth Bishop, *North & South*

Anthony West, *The Vintage*

Arthur Mizener, *The Far Side of Paradise*

Madison A. Cooper, Jr., *Sironia, Texas*

Charles Bracelen Flood, *Love Is a Bridge*

Milton Lott, *The Last Hunt*

Eugene Burdick, *The Ninth Wave*

Philip Roth, *Goodbye, Columbus*

William Brammer, *The Gay Place*

Clancy Sigal, *Going Away*

Edward Hoagland, *The Cat Man*

Ellen Douglas, *A Family's Affairs*

John Stewart Carter, *Full Fathom Five*

Margaret Walker, *Jubilee*

Berry Morgan, *Pursuit*

Robert Stone, *A Hall of Mirrors*

Willie Morris, *North Toward Home*

Georgia McKinley, *Follow the Running Grass*

Elizabeth Cullinan, *House of Gold*

Edward Hannibal, *Chocolate Days, Popsicle Weeks*

Helen Yglesias, *How She Died*

Henry Bromell, *The Slightest Distance*

Julia Markus, *Uncle*

Jean Strouse, *Alice James*

Patricia Hampl, *A Romantic Education*

W. P. Kinsella, *Shoeless Joe*

David Payne, *Confessions of a Taoist on Wall Street*

EMPEROR OF THE AIR

◆ ◆ ◆

Stories by Ethan Canin
Winner of a Houghton Mifflin
Literary Fellowship

◆

HOUGHTON MIFFLIN COMPANY
BOSTON ◆ 1988

Library of Congress Cataloging-in-Publication Data

Canin, Ethan.
Emperor of the air.
I. Title.
PS3553.A495E4 1988 813'.54 87-22540
ISBN 0-395-42976-5

Printed in the United States of America

P 10 9 8 7 6 5 4 3 2 1

Some of the stories in this collection have appeared elsewhere, in slightly different
form: "Emperor of the Air" in *The Atlantic* and *The Best American Short Stories 1985*;
"The Year of Getting to Know Us" and "Where We Are Now" in *The Atlantic*; "Lies"
in *San Francisco Stories* and the *Boston Globe Magazine*; "We Are Nighttime Travelers"
in *Esquire*; "Pitch Memory" in *Ploughshares*; "The Carnival Dog, the Buyer of
Diamonds" (under the title "Abe, Between Rounds") in *Redbook*; "Star Food" in
Chicago and *The Best American Short Stories 1986*.

The author is grateful for permission to quote lines from the following poems:
"Everything That Acts Is Actual," by Denise Levertov, in *Collected Earlier Poems,
1940–1960.* Copyright © 1957 by Denise Levertov Goodman. Reprinted by
permission of New Directions Publishing Corporation. "These," by William Carlos
Williams, in *Collected Poems, Volume I: 1909–1939.* Copyright 1938 by New
Directions Publishing Corporation. "The Love Song of J. Alfred Prufrock," by
T. S. Eliot, in *Collected Poems 1909–1962,* copyright 1936 by Harcourt Brace
Jovanovich, Inc.; copyright © 1963, 1964, by T. S. Eliot. Reprinted by
permission of the publisher.

For my parents, and my brother, Aram,
and for Barbara

The author is grateful to the Ingram Merrill Foundation, to James Michener and the Copernicus Society of America, and to the Henfield Foundation for support during the writing of this book.

Contents

EMPEROR
OF THE AIR

◆ ◆ ◆

LET ME TELL YOU who I am. I'm sixty-nine years old, live in the same house I was raised in, and have been the high school biology and astronomy teacher in this town so long that I have taught the grandson of one of my former students. I wear my father's wristwatch, which tells me it is past four-thirty in the morning, and though I have thought otherwise, I now think that hope is the essence of all good men.

My wife, Vera, and I have no children. This has enabled us to do a great many things in our lives: we have stood on the Great Wall of China, toured the Pyramid of Cheops, sunned in Lapland at midnight. Vera, who is near my age, is off on the Appalachian Trail. She has been gone two weeks and expects to be gone one more, on a trip on which a group of men and women, some of them half her age, are walking all the way through three states. Age, it seems, has left my wife alone. She ice-skates and hikes and will swim nude in a mountain lake. She does these things without me, however, for now my life has slowed. Last fall, as I pushed a lawn-mower around our yard, I felt a squeezing in my chest and a burst of pain in my shoulder, and I spent a week in a semi-private hospital room. A heart attack. Myocardial infarction, minor. I will no longer run for a train, and in my shirt pocket

I keep a small vial of nitroglycerine pills. In slow supermarket lines or traffic snarls I tell myself that impatience is not worth dying over, and last week, as I stood at the window and watched my neighbor, Mr. Pike, cross the yard toward our front door carrying a chain saw, I told myself that he was nothing but a doomed and hopeless man.

I had found the insects in my elm a couple of days before, the slim red line running from the ground up the long trunk and vanishing into the lower boughs. I brought out a magnifying glass to examine them—their shiny arthroderms, torsos elongated like drops of red liquid; their tiny legs, jointed and wiry, climbing the fissured bark. The morning I found them, Mr. Pike came over from next door and stood on our porch. "There's vermin in your elm," he said.

"I know," I said. "Come in."

"It's a shame, but I'll be frank: there's other trees on this block. I've got my own three elms to think of."

Mr. Pike is a builder, a thick and unpleasant man with whom I have rarely spoken. Though I had seen him at high school athletic events, the judgmental tilt to his jaw always suggested to me that he was merely watching for the players' mistakes. He is short, with thick arms and a thick neck and a son, Kurt, in whose bellicose shouts I can already begin to hear the thickness of his father. Mr. Pike owns or partly owns a construction company that erected a line of low prefabricated houses on the outskirts of town, on a plot I remember from my youth as having been razed by fire. Once, a plumber who was working on our basement pipes told me that Mr. Pike was a poor craftsman, a man who valued money over quality. The plumber, a man my age who kept his tools in a wooden chest, shook his head when he told me that Mr. Pike used plastic pipes in the houses he had built. "They'll last ten years," the plumber told me. "Then the seams will go and the walls and ceilings will start to fill with water." I myself had had little to do with Mr. Pike until he told me he wanted my elm cut down to protect the three saplings in his yard. Our houses are separated by a tall stand of rhododendron and ivy, so we don't see each other's private lives as most neighbors do. When we talked on the street, we spoke only about a football score or the incessant rain, and I had not been on his property since shortly after he moved in, when I had gone over to introduce myself and he had shown me the spot where, underneath his rolling back lawn, he planned to build a bomb shelter.

Last week he stood on my porch with the chain saw in his hands. "I've got young elms," he said. "I can't let them be infested."

"My tree is over two hundred years old."

"It's a shame," he said, showing me the saw, "but I'll be frank. I just wanted you to know I could have it cut down as soon as you give the word."

All week I had a hard time sleeping. I read Dickens in bed, heated cups of milk, but nothing worked. The elm was dying. Vera was gone, and I lay in bed thinking of the insects, of their miniature jaws carrying away heartwood. It was late summer, the nights were still warm, and sometimes I went outside in my nightclothes and looked up at the sky. I teach astronomy, as I have said, and though sometimes I try to see the stars as milky dots or pearls, they are forever arranged in my eye according to the astronomic charts. I stood by the elm and looked up at Ursa Minor and Lyra, at Cygnus and Corona Borealis. I went back inside, read, peeled an orange. I sat at the window and thought about the insects, and every morning at five a boy who had once taken my astronomy class rode by on his bicycle, whistling the national anthem, and threw the newspaper onto our porch.

Sometimes I heard them, chewing the heart of my splendid elm.

The day after I first found the insects I called a man at the tree nursery. He described them for me, the bodies like red droplets, the wiry legs; he told me their genus and species.

"Will they kill the tree?"

"They could."

"We can poison them, can't we?"

"Probably not," he said. He told me that once they were visible outside the bark they had already invaded the tree too thoroughly for pesticide. "To kill them," he said, "we would end up killing the tree."

"Does that mean the tree is dead?"

"No," he said. "It depends on the colony of insects. Sometimes they invade a tree but don't kill it, don't even weaken it. They eat the wood, but sometimes they eat it so slowly that the tree can replace it."

When Mr. Pike came over the next day, I told him this. "You're asking me to kill a two-hundred-and-fifty-year-old tree that otherwise wouldn't die for a long time."

"The tree's over eighty feet tall," he said.

"So?"

"It stands fifty-two feet from my house."

"Mr. Pike, it's older than the Liberty Bell."

"I don't want to be unpleasant," he said, "but a storm could blow twenty-eight feet of that tree through the wall of my house."

"How long have you lived in that house?"

He looked at me, picked at his tooth. "You know."

"Four years," I said. "I was living here when a czar ruled Russia. An elm grows one quarter inch in width each year, when it's still growing. That tree is four feet thick, and it has yet to chip the paint on either your house or mine."

"It's sick," he said. "It's a sick tree. It could fall."

"Could," I said. "It *could* fall."

"It very well *might* fall."

We looked at each other for a moment. Then he averted his eyes, and with his right hand adjusted something on his watch. I looked at his wrist. The watch had a shiny metal band, with the hours, minutes, seconds, blinking in the display.

The next day he was back on my porch.

"We can plant another one," he said.

"What?"

"We can plant another tree. After we cut the elm, we can plant a new one."

"Do you have any idea how long it would take to grow a tree like that one?"

"You can buy trees half-grown. They bring them in on a truck and replant them."

"Even a half-grown tree would take a century to reach the size of the elm. A century."

He looked at me. Then he shrugged, turned around, and went back down the steps. I sat down in the open doorway. A century. What would be left of the earth in a century? I didn't think I was a sentimental man, and I don't weep at plays or movies, but certain moments have always been peculiarly moving for me, and the mention of a century was one. There have been others. Standing out of the way on a fall evening, as couples and families converge on the concert hall from the radiating footpaths, has always filled me with a longing, though I don't know for what. I have taught the life of the simple hydra that is drawn, for no reasons it could ever understand, toward the bright surface of the water, and the spectacle of a thousand human beings organizing themselves into a single room to hear the quartets of Beethoven is as moving to me as birth or death. I feel the same way during the passage in an automobile across a cantilever span above the Mississippi, mother of rivers. These moments overwhelm me, and sitting on the porch that day as Mr. Pike retreated up the footpath, paused at the elm, and then went back into his house, I felt my life open up and present itself to me.

When he had gone back into his house I went out to the elm and studied the insects, which emerged from a spot in the grass and disappeared above my sight, in the lowest branches. Their line was dense and unbroken. I went inside and found yesterday's newspaper, which I rolled up and brought back out. With it I slapped up and down the trunk until the line was in chaos. I slapped until the newspaper was wet and tearing; with my fingernails I squashed stragglers between the narrow crags of bark. I stamped the sod where they emerged, dug my shoe tip into their underground tunnels. When my breathing became painful, I stopped and sat on the ground. I closed my eyes until the pulse in my neck was calm, and I sat there, mildly triumphant, master at last. After a while I looked up again at the tree and found the line perfectly restored.

That afternoon I mixed a strong insect poison, which I brought outside and painted around the bottom of the trunk. Mr. Pike came out onto his steps to watch. He walked down, stood on the sidewalk behind me, made little chuckling noises. "There's no poison that'll work," he whispered.

But that evening, when I came outside, the insects were gone. The trunk was bare. I ran my finger around the circumference. I rang Mr. Pike's doorbell and we went out and stood by the tree together. He felt in the notches of the bark, scratched bits of earth from the base. "I'll be damned," he said.

When I was a boy in this town, the summers were hot and the forest to the north and east often dried to the point where the undergrowth, not fit to compete with the deciduous trees for groundwater, turned crackling brown. The shrubbery became as fragile as straw, and the summer I was sixteen the forest ignited. A sheet of flame raced and bellowed day and night as loud as a fleet of propeller planes. Whole families gathered in the street and evacuation plans were made, street routes drawn out beneath the night sky, which, despite the ten miles' distance to the fire, shone with orange light. My father had a wireless with which he communicated to the fire lines. He stayed up all night and promised that he would wake the neighbors if the wind changed or the fire otherwise turned toward town. That night the wind held, and by morning a firebreak the width of a street had been cut. My father took me down to see it the next day, a ribbon of cleared land as bare as if it had been drawn with a razor. Trees had been felled, the underbrush sickled down and removed. We stood at the edge of the cleared land, the town behind us, and watched the fire. Then we got into my father's Plymouth and drove as close as we were allowed. A fireman near the flames had been asphyxiated, someone said, when the cone of fire had turned abruptly and sucked up all the oxygen in the air. My father explained to me how a flame breathed oxygen like a man. We got out of the car. The heat curled the hair on our arms and turned the ends of our eyelashes white.

My father was a pharmacist and had taken me to the fire out of curiosity. Anything scientific interested him. He kept tide tables and collected the details of nature—butterflies and moths, seeds, wildflowers—and stored them in glass-fronted cases, which he leaned against the stone wall of our cellar. One summer he taught me the constellations of the Northern Hemisphere. We went outside at night, and as the summer progressed he showed me how to find Perseus and Boötes and Andromeda, how some of the brightest stars illuminated Lyra and Aquila, how, though the constellations proceed with the seasons, Polaris remains most fixed and is thus the set point of a mariner's navigation. He taught me the night sky, and I find now that this is rare knowledge. Later, when I taught astronomy, my students rarely cared about the silicon or iron on the sun, but when I spoke of Cepheus or Lacerta, they were silent and attended my words. At a party now I can always find a drinking husband who will come outside with me and sip cognac while I point out the stars and say their names.

That day, as I stood and watched the fire, I thought the flames were as loud and powerful as the sea, and that evening, when we were home, I went out to the front yard and climbed the elm to watch the forest burn. Climbing the elm was forbidden me, because the lowest limbs even then were well above my reach and because my father believed that anybody lucky enough to make it up into the lower boughs would almost certainly fall on the way down. But I knew how to climb it anyway. I had done it before, when my parents were gone. I had never made it as far as the first limbs, but I had learned the knobs and handholds on which, with balance and strength, I could climb to within a single jump of the boughs. The jump frightened me, however, and I had never attempted it. To reach the boughs one had to gather strength and leap upward into the air, propelled only by the purchase of feet and hands on the small juttings of bark. It was a terrible risk. I could no more imagine myself making this leap than I could imagine diving headlong from a coastal cliff into the sea. I was an adventurous youth, as I was later an adventurous man, but all my adventures had a quality about them of safety and planned success. This is still true. In Ethiopia I have photographed a lioness with her cubs; along the Barrier Reef I have dived among barracuda and scorpion fish—but these things have never frightened me. In my life I have done few things that have frightened me.

That night, though, I made the leap into the lower boughs of the elm. My parents were inside the house, and I made my way upward until I crawled out of the leaves onto a narrow top branch and looked around me at a world that on two sides was entirely red and orange with flame. After a time I came back down and went inside to sleep, but that night the wind changed. My father woke us, and we gathered outside on the street with all the other families on our block. People carried blankets filled with the treasures of their lives. One woman wore a fur coat, though the air was suffused with ash and was as warm as an afternoon. My father stood on the hood of a car and spoke. He had heard through the radio that the fire had leaped the break, that a house on the eastern edge of town was in full flame, and, as we all could feel, that the wind was strong and blowing straight west. He told the families to finish loading their cars and leave as soon as possible. Though the fire was still across town, he said, the air was filling with smoke so rapidly that breathing would soon be difficult. He got down off the car and we went inside to gather things together. We had an RCA radio in our living room and a set of Swiss china in my mother's cupboard, but my father instead loaded a box with the *Encyclopaedia Britannica* and carried up from the basement the heavy glass cases that contained his species chart of the North American butterflies. We carried these things outside to the Plymouth. When we returned, my mother was standing in the doorway.

"This is my home," she said.

"We're in a hurry," said my father.

"This is my home, this is my children's home. I'm not leaving."

My father stood on the porch looking at her. "Stay here," he said to me. Then he took my mother's arm and they went into the house. I stood on the steps outside, and when my father came out again in a few minutes, he was alone, just as when we drove west that night and slept with the rest of our neighborhood on army cots in the high school gym in the next town, we were alone. My mother had stayed behind.

Nothing important came of this. That night the wind

calmed and the burning house was extinguished; the next day a heavy rain wet the fire and it was put out. Everybody came home, and the settled ash was swept from the houses and walkways into black piles in the street. I mention the incident now only because it points out, I think, what I have always lacked: I inherited none of my mother's moral stubbornness. In spite of my age, still, arriving on foot at a crosswalk where the light is red but no cars are in sight, I'm thrown into confusion. My decisions never seem to engage the certainty that I had hoped to enjoy late in my life. But I was adamant and angry when Mr. Pike came to my door. The elm was ancient and exquisite: we could not let it die.

Now, though, the tree was safe. I examined it in the morning, in the afternoon, in the evening, and with a lantern at night. The bark was clear. I slept.

The next morning Mr. Pike was at my door.

"Good morning, neighbor," I said.

"They're back."

"They can't be."

"They are. Look," he said, and walked out to the tree. He pointed up to the first bough.

"You probably can't see them," he said, "but I can. They're up there, a whole line of them."

"They couldn't be."

"They sure are. Listen," he said, "I don't want to be unpleasant, but I'll be frank."

That evening he left a note in our mail slot. It said that he had contacted the authorities, who had agreed to enforce the cutting of the tree if I didn't do it myself. I read the note in the kitchen. Vera had been cooking some Indian chicken before she left for the Appalachian Trail, and on the counter was a big jar filled with flour and spices that she shook pieces of chicken in. I read Mr. Pike's note again. Then I got a fishing knife and a flashlight from the closet, emptied Vera's jar, and went outside with these things to the elm. The street was quiet. I made a few calculations, and then with the knife cut the bark. Nothing. I had to do it only a couple more times, however, before I hit the mark and, sure enough, the tree sprouted insects. Tiny red bugs shot crazily from the slit in the bark. I touched my finger there and they spread in an instant all over my hand and up my arm. I had to shake them off. Then I opened the jar, laid the fishing knife out from the opening like a bridge, and touched the blade to the slit in the tree. They scrambled up the knife and began to fill the jar as fast as a trickling spring. After a few minutes I pulled out the knife, closed the lid, and went back into the house.

Mr. Pike is my neighbor, and so I felt a certain remorse. What I contemplated, however, was not going to kill the elms. It was going to save them. If Mr. Pike's trees were infested, they would still more than likely live, and he would no longer want mine chopped down. This is the nature of the world. In the dark house, feeling half like a criminal and half like a man of mercy, my heart arrhythmic in anticipation, I went upstairs to prepare. I put on black pants and a black shirt. I dabbed shoe polish on my cheeks, my neck, my wrists, the backs of my hands. Over my white hair I stretched a tight black cap. Then I walked downstairs. I picked up the jar and the flashlight and went outside into the night.

I have always enjoyed gestures—never failing to bow, for example, when I finished dancing with a woman—but one attribute I have acquired with age is the ability to predict when I am about to act foolishly. As I slid calmly into the shadowy cavern behind our side yard rhododendron and paused to catch my breath, I thought that perhaps I had better go back inside and get into my bed. But then I decided to go through with it. As I stood there in the shadow of the swaying rhododendron, waiting to pass into the back yard of my neighbor, I thought of Hannibal and Napoleon and MacArthur. I tested my flashlight and shook the jar, which made a soft colliding sound as if it were filled with rice. A light was on in the Pikes' living room, but the alley between our houses was dark. I passed through.

The Pikes' yard is large, larger than ours, and slopes twice within its length, so that the lawn that night seemed like a dark, furrowed flag stretching back to the three elms. I paused at the border of the driveway, where the grass began, and looked out at the young trees outlined by the lighted houses behind them. In what strange ways, I thought, do our lives turn. Then I got down on my hands and knees. Staying along the fence that separates our yards, I crawled toward the back of the Pikes' lawn. In my life I have not crawled a lot. With Vera I have gone spelunking in the limestone caves of southern Minnesota, but there the crawling was obligate, and as we made our way along the narrow, wet channel into the heart of the rock, I felt a strange grace in my knees and elbows. The channel was hideously narrow, and my life depended on the sureness of my limbs. Now, in the Pikes' yard, my knees felt arthritic and torn. I made my way along the driveway toward the young elms against the back fence. The grass was wet and the water dampened my trousers. I was hurrying as best I could across the open lawn, the insect-filled jar in my hand, the flashlight in my pocket, when I put my palm on something cement. I stopped and looked down. In the dim light I saw what looked like the hatch door on a submarine. Round, the size of a manhole, marked with a fluorescent cross—oh, Mr. Pike, I didn't think you'd do it. I put down the jar and felt for the handle in the dark, and when I found it I braced myself and turned. I certainly didn't expect it to give, but it did, circling once, twice, around in my grasp and loosening like the lid of a bottle. I pulled the hatch and up it came. Then I picked up the insects, felt with my feet for the ladder inside, and went down.

I still planned to deposit the insects on his trees, but something about crime is contagious. I knew that what I was doing was foolish and that it increased the risk of being caught, but as I descended the ladder into Mr. Pike's bomb shelter, I could barely distinguish fear from elation. At the bottom of the ladder I switched on the flashlight. The room was round, the ceiling and floor were concrete, and against the wall stood a cabinet of metal shelves filled with canned foods. On one shelf were a dictionary and some magazines. Oh, Mr. Pike. I thought of his sapling elms, of the roots making their steady, blind way through the earth; I thought of his houses ten years from now, when the pipes cracked and the ceilings began to pool with water. What a hopeless man he seemed to me then, how small and afraid.

I stood thinking about him, and after a moment I heard a door close in the house. I climbed the ladder and peeked out under the hatch. There on the porch stood Kurt and Mr. Pike. As I watched, they came down off the steps, walked over and stood on the grass near me. I could see the watch blinking on Mr. Pike's wrist. I lowered my head. They were silent, and I wondered what Mr. Pike would do if he found me in his bomb shelter. He was thickly built, as I have said, but I didn't think he was a violent man. One afternoon I had watched as Kurt slammed the front door of their house and ran down the steps onto the lawn, where he stopped and threw an object—an ashtray, I think it was—right through the front window of the house. When the glass shattered, he ran, and Mr. Pike soon appeared on the front steps. The reason I say that he is not a violent man is that I saw something beyond anger, perhaps a certain doom, in his posture as he went back inside that afternoon and began cleaning up the glass with a broom. I watched him through the broken front window of their house.

How would I explain to him, though, the bottle of mad

insects I now held? I could have run then, I suppose, made a break up and out of the shelter while their backs were turned. I could have been out the driveway and across the street without their recognizing me. But there was, of course, my heart. I moved back down the ladder. As I descended and began to think about a place to hide my insects, I heard Mr. Pike speak. I climbed back up the ladder. When I looked out under the hatch, I saw the two of them, backs toward me, pointing at the sky. Mr. Pike was sighting something with his finger, and Kurt followed. Then I realized that he was pointing out the constellations, but that he didn't know what they were and was making up their names as he spoke. His voice was not fanciful. It was direct and scientific, and he was lying to his son about what he knew. "These," he said, "these are the Mermaid's Tail, and south you can see the three peaks of Mount Olympus, and then the sword that belongs to the Emperor of the Air." I looked where he was pointing. It was late summer, near midnight, and what he had described was actually Cygnus's bright tail and the outstretched neck of Pegasus.

Presently he ceased speaking, and after a time they walked back across the lawn and went into the house. The light in the kitchen went on, then off. I stepped from my hiding place. I suppose I could have continued with my mission, but the air was calm, it was a perfect and still night, and my plan, I felt, had been interrupted. In my hand the jar felt large and dangerous. I crept back across the lawn, staying in the shadows of the ivy and rhododendron along the fence, until I was in the driveway between our two houses. In the side window of the Pikes' house a light was on. I paused at a point where the angle allowed me a view through the glass, down the hallway, and through an open door into the living room. Mr. Pike and Kurt were sitting together on a brown couch against the far wall of the room, watching television.

I came up close to the window and peered through. Though I knew this was foolish, that any neighbor, any man walking his dog at night, would have thought me a burglar in my black clothing, I stayed and watched. The light was on inside, it was dark around me, and I knew I could look in without being seen. Mr. Pike had his hand on Kurt's shoulder. Every so often when they laughed at something on the screen, he moved his hand up and tousled Kurt's hair, and the sight of this suddenly made me feel the way I do on the bridge across the Mississippi River. When he put his hand on Kurt's hair again, I moved out of the shadows and went back to my own house.

I wanted to run, or kick a ball, or shout a soliloquy into the night. I could have stepped up on a car hood then and lured the Pikes, the paper boy, all the neighbors, out into the night. I could have spoken about the laboratory of a biology teacher, about the rows of specimen jars. How could one not hope here? At three weeks the human embryo has gill arches on its neck, like a fish; at six weeks, amphibians' webs still connect its blunt fingers. Miracles. This is true everywhere in nature. The evolution of five hundred million years is mimicked in each gestation: birds that in the egg look like fish; fish that emerge like their spineless, leaflike ancestors. What it is to study life! Anybody who had seen a cell divide could have invented religion.

I sat down on the porch steps and looked at the elm. After a while I stood up and went inside. With turpentine I cleaned the shoe polish from my face, and then I went upstairs. I got into bed. For an hour or two I lay there, sleepless, hot, my thoughts racing, before I gave up and went to the bedroom window. The jar, which I had brought up with me, stood on the sill, and I saw that the insects were either asleep or dead. I opened the window then and emptied them down onto the lawn, and at that moment, as they rained away into the night, glinting and cascading, I thought of asking Vera for a child. I knew it was not possible, but I considered it anyway. Standing there at the window, I thought of Vera, ageless, in forest boots and shorts, perspiring through a flannel blouse as she dipped drinking water from an Appalachian stream. What had we, she and I? The night was calm, dark. Above me Polaris blinked.

I tried going to sleep again. I lay in bed for a time, and then gave up and went downstairs. I ate some crackers. I drank two glasses of bourbon. I sat at the window and looked out at the front yard. Then I got up and went outside and looked up at the stars, and I tried to see them for their beauty and mystery. I thought of billions of tons of exploding gases, hydrogen and helium, red giants, supernovas. In places they were as dense as clouds. I thought of magnesium and silicon and iron. I tried to see them out of their constellatory order, but it was like trying to look at a word without reading it, and I stood there in the night unable to scramble the patterns. Some clouds had blown in and begun to cover Auriga and Taurus. I was watching them begin to spread and refract moonlight when I heard the paper boy whistling the national anthem. When he reached me, I was standing by the elm, still in my nightclothes, unshaven, a little drunk.

"I want you to do something for me," I said.

"Sir?"

"I'm an old man and I want you to do something for me. Put down your bicycle," I said. "Put down your bicycle and look up at the stars."

THE YEAR
OF GETTING TO
KNOW US

◆ ◆ ◆

I TOLD MY FATHER not to worry, that love is what matters, and that in the end, when he is loosed from his body, he can look back and say without blinking that he did all right by me, his son, and that I loved him.

And he said, "Don't talk about things you know nothing about."

We were in San Francisco, in a hospital room. IV tubes were plugged into my father's arms; little round Band-Aids were on his chest. Next to his bed was a table with a vase of yellow roses and a card that my wife, Anne, had brought him. On the front of the card was a photograph of a golf green. On the wall above my father's head an electric monitor traced his heartbeat. He was watching the news on a TV that stood in the corner next to his girlfriend, Lorraine. Lorraine was reading a magazine.

I was watching his heartbeat. It seemed all right to me: the blips made steady peaks and drops, moved across the screen, went out at one end, and then came back at the other. It seemed that this was all a heart could do. I'm an English teacher, though, and I don't know much about it.

"It looks strong," I'd said to my mother that afternoon over the phone. She was in Pasadena. "It's going right across, pretty steady. Big bumps. Solid."

"Is he eating all right?"

"I think so."

"Is *she* there?"

"Is Lorraine here, you mean?"

She paused. "Yes, Lorraine."

"No," I said. "She's not."

"Your poor father," she whispered.

I'm an only child, and I grew up in a big wood-frame house on Huron Avenue in Pasadena, California. The house had three empty bedrooms and in the back yard a section of grass that had been stripped and leveled, then seeded and mowed like a putting green. Twice a week a Mexican gardener came to trim it, wearing special moccasins my father had bought him. They had soft hide soles that left no imprints.

My father was in love with golf. He played seven times every week and talked about the game as if it were a science that he was about to figure out. "Cut through the outer rim for a high iron," he used to say at dinner, looking out the window into the yard while my mother passed him the carved-wood salad bowl, or "In hot weather hit a high-compression ball." When conversations paused, he made little putting motions with his hands. He was a top amateur and in another situation might have been a pro. When I was sixteen, the year I was arrested, he let me caddie for the first time. Before that all I knew about golf was his clubs—the Spalding made-to-measure woods and irons, Dynamiter sand wedge, St. Andrews putter—which he kept in an Abercrombie & Fitch bag in the trunk of his Lincoln, and the white leather shoes with long tongues and screw-in spikes, which he stored upside down in the hall closet. When he wasn't playing, he covered the club heads with socks that had little yellow dingo balls on the ends.

He never taught me to play. I was a decent athlete—could run, catch, throw a perfect spiral—but he never took me to the golf course. In the summer he played every day. Sometimes my mother asked if he would take me along with him. "Why should I?" he answered. "Neither of us would like it."

Every afternoon after work he played nine holes; he played eighteen on Saturday, and nine again on Sunday morning. On Sunday afternoon, at four o'clock, he went for a drive by himself in his white Lincoln Continental. Nobody was allowed to come with him on the drives. He was usually gone for a couple of hours. "Today I drove in the country," he would say at dinner, as he put out his cigarette, or "This afternoon I looked at the ocean," and we were to take from this that he had driven north on the coastal highway. He almost never said more, and across our blue-and-white tablecloth, when I looked at him, my silent father, I imagined in his eyes a pure gaze with which he read the waves and currents of the sea. He had made a fortune in business and owed it to being able to see the truth in any situation. For this reason, he said, he liked to drive with all the windows down. When he returned from his trips his face was red from the wind and his thinning hair lay fitfully on his head. My mother baked on Sunday afternoons while he was gone, walnut pies or macaroons that she prepared on the kitchen counter, which looked out over his putting green.

I teach English in a high school now, and my wife, Anne, is a journalist. I've played golf a half-dozen times in ten years and don't like it any more than most beginners, though the two or three times I've hit a drive that sails, that takes flight with its own power, I've felt something that I think must be unique to the game. These were the drives my father used to hit. Explosions off the tee, bird flights. But golf isn't my game, and it never has been, and I wouldn't think about it at all if not for my father.

Anne and I were visiting in California, first my mother, in Los Angeles, and then my father and Lorraine, north in Sausalito, and Anne suggested that I ask him to play nine holes one morning. She'd been wanting me to talk to him. It's part of the project we've started, part of her theory of what's wrong—although I don't think that much is. She had told me that twenty-five years changes things, and since we had the time, why not go out to California.

She said, "It's not too late to talk to him."

My best friend in high school was named Nickie Apple. Nickie had a thick chest and a voice that had been damaged somehow, made a little hoarse, and sometimes people thought he was twenty years old. He lived in a four-story house that had a separate floor for the kids. It was the top story, and his father, who was divorced and a lawyer, had agreed never to come up there. That was where we sat around after school. Because of the agreement, no parents were there, only kids. Nine or ten of us, usually. Some of them had slept the night on the big pillows that were scattered against the walls: friends of his older brothers', in Stetson hats and flannel shirts; girls I had never seen before.

Nickie and I went to Shrier Academy, where all the students carried around blue-and-gray notebooks embossed with the school's heraldic seal. SUMUS PRIMI the seal said. Our gray wool sweaters said it; our green exam books said it; the rear window decal my mother brought home said it. My father wouldn't put the sticker on the Lincoln, so she pressed it onto the window above her kitchen sink instead. SUMUS IMIꓤꟼ I read whenever I washed my hands. At Shrier we learned Latin in the eighth grade and art history in the ninth, and in the tenth I started getting into some trouble. Little

things: cigarettes, graffiti. Mr. Goldman, the student counselor, called my mother in for a premonition visit. "I have a
premonition about Leonard," he told her in the counseling
office one afternoon in the warm October when I was sixteen.
The office was full of plants and had five floor-to-ceiling
windows that let in sun like a greenhouse. They looked
over grassy, bushless knolls. "I just have a feeling about
him."

That October he started talking to me about it. He called
me in and asked me why I was friends with Nickie Apple, a
boy going nowhere. I was looking out the big windows,
opening and closing my fists beneath the desk top. He said,
"Lenny, you're a bright kid—what are you trying to tell
us?" And I said, "Nothing. I'm not trying to tell you anything."

Then we started stealing, Nickie and I. He did it first, and
took things I didn't expect: steaks, expensive cuts that we
cooked on a grill by the window in the top story of his house;
garden machinery; luggage. We didn't sell it and we didn't
use it, but every afternoon we went someplace new. In November he distracted a store clerk and I took a necklace that
we thought was diamonds. In December we went for a ride
in someone else's car, and over Christmas vacation, when only
gardeners were on the school grounds, we threw ten rocks,
one by one, as if we'd paid for them at a carnival stand,
through the five windows in Mr. Goldman's office.

"You look like a train station," I said to my father as he lay
in the hospital bed. "All those lines coming and going everywhere."

He looked at me. I put some things down, tried to make
a little bustle. I could see Anne standing in the hall just
beyond the door.

"Are you comfortable, Dad?"

"What do you mean, 'comfortable'? My heart's full of holes, leaking all over the place. Am I comfortable? No, I'm dying."

"You're not dying," I said, and I sat down next to him. "You'll be swinging the five iron in two weeks."

I touched one of the tubes in his arm. Where it entered the vein, the needle disappeared under a piece of tape. I hated the sight of this. I moved the bedsheets a little bit, tucked them in. Anne had wanted me to be alone with him. She was in the hall, waiting to head off Lorraine.

"What's the matter with her?" he asked, pointing at Anne.

"She thought we might want to talk."

"What's so urgent?"

Anne and I had discussed it the night before. "Tell him what you feel," she said. "Tell him you love him." We were eating dinner in a fish restaurant. "Or if you don't love him, tell him you don't."

"Look, Pop," I said now.

"What?"

I was forty-two years old. We were in a hospital and he had tubes in his arms. All kinds of everything: needles, air, tape. I said it again.

"Look, Pop."

Anne and I have seen a counselor, who told me that I had to learn to accept kindness from people. He saw Anne and me together, then Anne alone, then me. Children's toys were scattered on the floor of his office. "You sound as if you don't want to let people near you," he said. "Right?"

"I'm a reasonably happy man," I answered.

I hadn't wanted to see the counselor. Anne and I have been married seven years, and sometimes I think the history of marriage can be written like this: People Want Too Much. Anne and I have suffered no plague; we sleep late two mornings a week; we laugh at most of the same things; we have a decent house in a suburb of Boston, where, after the commuter traffic has eased, a quiet descends and the world is at peace. She writes for a newspaper, and I teach the children of lawyers and insurance men. At times I'm alone, and need to be alone; at times she does too. But I can always count on a moment, sometimes once in a day, sometimes more, when I see her patting down the sheets on the bed, or watering the front window violets, and I am struck by the good fortune of my life.

Still, Anne says I don't feel things.

It comes up at dinner, outside in the yard, in airports as we wait for planes. You don't let yourself feel, she tells me; and I tell her that I think it's a crazy thing, all this talk about feeling. What do the African Bushmen say? They say, Will we eat tomorrow? Will there be rain?

When I was sixteen, sitting in the back seat of a squad car, the policeman stopped in front of our house on Huron Avenue, turned around against the headrest, and asked me if I was sure this was where I lived.

"Yes, sir," I said.

He spoke through a metal grate. "Your daddy owns this house?"

"Yes, sir."

"But for some reason you don't like windows."

He got out and opened my door, and we walked up the porch steps. The swirling lights on the squad car were making crazy patterns in the French panes of the living room bays. He knocked. "What's your daddy do?"

I heard lights snapping on, my mother moving through the house. "He's in business," I said. "But he won't be home now." The policeman wrote something on his notepad. I saw my mother's eye through the glass in the door, and then the locks were being unlatched, one by one, from the top.

* * *

When Anne and I came to California to visit, we stayed at my mother's for three days. On her refrigerator door was a calendar with men's names marked on it—dinner dates, theater—and I knew this was done for our benefit. My mother has been alone for fifteen years. She's still thin, and her eyes still water, and I noticed that books were lying open all through the house. Thick paperbacks—*Doctor Zhivago, The Thorn Birds*—in the bathroom and the studio and the bedroom. We never mentioned my father, but at the end of our stay, when we had packed the car for our drive north along the coast, after she'd hugged us both and we'd backed out of the driveway, she came down off the lawn into the street, her arms crossed over her chest, leaned into the window, and said, "You might say hello to your father for me."

We made the drive north on Highway 1. We passed mission towns, fields of butter lettuce, long stretches of pumpkin farms south of San Francisco. It was the first time we were going to see my father with Lorraine. She was a hairdresser. He'd met her a few years after coming north, and one of the first things they'd done together was take a trip around the world. We got postcards from the Nile delta and Bangkok. When I was young, my father had never taken us out of California.

His house in Sausalito was on a cliff above a finger of San Francisco Bay. A new Lincoln stood in the carport. In his bedroom was a teak-framed king-size waterbed, and on the walls were bits of African artwork—opium pipes, metal figurines. Lorraine looked the same age as Anne. One wall of the living room was glass, and after the first night's dinner, while we sat on the leather sofa watching tankers and yachts move under the Golden Gate Bridge, my father put down his Scotch and water, touched his jaw, and said, "Lenny, call Dr. Farmer."

It was his second one. The first had been two years earlier, on the golf course in Monterey, where he'd had to kneel, then sit, then lie down on the fairway.

At dinner the night after I was arrested, my mother introduced her idea. "We're going to try something," she said. She had brought out a chicken casserole, and it was steaming in front of her. "That's what we're going to do. Max, are you listening? This next year, starting tonight, is going to be the year of getting to know us better." She stopped speaking and dished my father some chicken.

"What do you mean?" I asked.

"I mean it will be to a small extent a theme year. Nothing that's going to change every day of our lives, but in this next year I thought we'd all make an attempt to get to know each other better. Especially you, Leonard. Dad and I are going to make a better effort to know you."

"I'm not sure what you mean," said my father.

"All kinds of things, Max. We'll go to movies together, and Lenny can throw a party here at the house. And I personally would like to take a trip, all of us together, to the American Southwest."

"Sounds all right to me," I said.

"And Max," she said, "you can take Lenny with you to play golf. For example." She looked at my father.

"Neither of us would like it," he said.

"Lenny never sees you."

I looked out the window. The trees were turning, dropping their leaves onto the putting green. I didn't care what he said, one way or the other. My mother spooned a chicken thigh onto my plate and covered it with sauce. "All right," my father said. "He can caddie."

"And as preparation for our trip," my mother said, "can you take him on your Sunday rides?"

My father took off his glasses. "The Southwest," he said,

wiping the lenses with a napkin, "is exactly like any other part of the country."

Anne had an affair once with a man she met on an assignment. He was young, much younger than either of us—in his late twenties, I would say from the one time I saw him. I saw them because one day on the road home I passed Anne's car in the lot of a Denny's restaurant. I parked around the block and went in to surprise her. I took a table at the back, but from my seat in the corner I didn't realize for several minutes that the youngish-looking woman leaning forward and whispering to the man with a beard was my wife.

I didn't get up and pull the man out with me into the parking lot, or even join them at the table, as I have since thought might have been a good idea. Instead I sat and watched them. I could see that under the table they were holding hands. His back was to me, and I noticed that it was broad, as mine is not. I remember thinking that she probably liked this broadness. Other than that, though, I didn't feel very much. I ordered another cup of coffee just to hear myself talk, but my voice wasn't quavering or fearful. When the waitress left, I took out a napkin and wrote on it, "You are a forty-year-old man with no children and your wife is having an affair." Then I put some money on the table and left the restaurant.

"I think we should see somebody," Anne said to me a few weeks later. It was a Sunday morning, and we were eating breakfast on the porch.

"About what?" I asked.

On a Sunday afternoon when I was sixteen I went out to the garage with a plan my mother had given me. That morning my father had washed the Lincoln. He had detergent-scrubbed the finish and then sun-dried it on Huron Avenue, so that in the workshop light of the garage its highlights shone. The windshield molding, the grille, the chrome side markers, had been cloth-dried to erase water spots. The keys hung from their magnetic sling near the door to the kitchen. I took them out and opened the trunk. Then I hung them up again and sat on the rear quarter panel to consider what to do. It was almost four o'clock. The trunk of my father's car was large enough for a half-dozen suitcases and had been up-holstered in a gray medium-pile carpet that was cut to hug the wheel wells and the spare-tire berth. In one corner, fastened down by straps, was his toolbox, and along the back lay the golf bag. In the shadows the yellow dingos of the club socks looked like baby chicks. He was going to come out in a few minutes. I reached in, took off four of the club socks, and made a pillow for my head. Then I stepped into the trunk. The shocks bounced once and stopped. I lay down with my head propped on the quarter panel and my feet resting in the taillight berth, and then I reached up, slammed down the trunk, and was in the dark.

This didn't frighten me. When I was very young, I liked to sleep with the shades drawn and the door closed so that no light entered my room. I used to hold my hand in front of my eyes and see if I could imagine its presence. It was too dark to see anything. I was blind then, lying in my bed, listening for every sound. I used to move my hand back and forth, close to my eyes, until I had the sensation that it was there but had in some way been amputated. I had heard of soldiers who had lost limbs but still felt them attached. Now I held my open hand before my eyes. It was dense black inside the trunk, colorless, without light.

When my father started the car, all the sounds were huge, magnified as if they were inside my own skull. The metal scratched, creaked, slammed when he got in; the bolt of the starter shook all the way through to the trunk; the idle rose and leveled; then the gears changed and the car lurched. I heard the garage door glide up. Then it curled into its housing, bumped once, began descending again. The seams of the trunk lid lightened in the sun. We were in the street now, heading downhill. I lay back and felt the road, listened to the gravel pocking in the wheel wells.

I followed our route in my mind. Left off Huron onto Telscher, where the car bottomed in the rain gulley as we turned, then up the hill to Santa Ana. As we waited for the light, the idle made its change, shifting down, so that below my head I heard the individual piston blasts in the exhaust pipe. Left on Santa Ana, counting the flat stretches where I felt my father tap the brakes, numbering the intersections as we headed west toward the ocean. I heard cars pull up next to us, accelerate, slow down, make turns. Bits of gravel echoed inside the quarter panels. I pulled off more club socks and enlarged my pillow. We slowed down, stopped, and then we accelerated, the soft piston explosions becoming a hiss as we turned onto the Pasadena freeway.

"Dad's rides," my mother had said to me the night before, as I lay in bed, "would be a good way for him to get to know you." It was the first week of the year of getting to know us better. She was sitting at my desk.

"But he won't let me go," I said.

"You're right." She moved some things around on a shelf. The room wasn't quite dark, and I could see the outline of her white blouse. "I talked to Mr. Goldman," she said.

"Mr. Goldman doesn't know me."

"He says you're angry." My mother stood up, and I watched her white blouse move to the window. She pulled back the shade until a triangle of light from the streetlamp fell on my sheets. "Are you angry?"

"I don't know," I said. "I don't think so."

"I don't think so either." She replaced the shade, came over and kissed me on the forehead, and then went out into the hall. In the dark I looked for my hand.

A few minutes later the door opened again. She put her head in. "If he won't let you come," she said, "sneak along."

On the freeway the thermal seams whizzed and popped in my ears. The ride had smoothed out now, as the shocks settled into the high speed, hardly dipping on curves, muffling everything as if we were under water. As far as I could tell, we were still driving west, toward the ocean. I sat halfway up and rested my back against the golf bag. I could see shapes now inside the trunk. When we slowed down and the blinker went on, I attempted bearings, but the sun was the same in all directions and the trunk lid was without shadow. We braked hard. I felt the car leave the freeway. We made turns. We went straight. Then more turns, and as we slowed down and I was stretching out, uncurling my body along the diagonal, we made a sharp right onto gravel and pulled over and stopped.

My father opened the door. The car dipped and rocked, shuddered. The engine clicked. Then the passenger door opened. I waited.

If I heard her voice today, twenty-six years later, I would recognize it.

"Angel," she said.

I heard the weight of their bodies sliding across the back seat, first hers, then his. They weren't three feet away. I curled up, crouched into the low space between the golf bag and the back of the passenger compartment. There were two firm points in the cushion where it was displaced. As I lay there, I went over the voice again in my head: it was nobody I knew. I heard a laugh from her, and then something low from him. I felt the shift of the trunk's false rear, and then, as I lay behind them, I heard the contact: the crinkle of clothing, arms wrapping, and the half-delicate, muscular sounds.

It was like hearing a television in the next room. His voice once more, and then the rising of their breath, slow; a minute of this, maybe another; then shifting again, the friction of cloth on the leather seat and the car's soft rocking. "Dad," I whispered. Then rocking again; my father's sudden panting, harder and harder, his half-words. The car shook violently. "Dad," I whispered. I shouted, "Dad!"

The door opened.

His steps kicked up gravel. I heard jingling metal, the sound of the key in the trunk lock. He was standing over me in an explosion of light.

He said, "Put back the club socks."

I did and got out of the car to stand next to him. He rubbed his hands down the front of his shirt.

"What the hell," he said.

"I was in the trunk."

"I know," he said. "What the goddamn."

The year I graduated from college, I found a job teaching junior high school in Boston. The school was a cement building with small windows well up from the street, and dark classrooms in which I spent a lot of time maintaining discipline. In the middle of an afternoon that first winter a boy knocked on my door to tell me I had a phone call. I knew who it was going to be.

"Dad's gone," my mother said.

He'd taken his things in the Lincoln, she told me, and driven away that morning before dawn. On the kitchen table he'd left a note and some cash. "A lot of cash," my mother added, lowering her voice. "Twenty thousand dollars."

I imagined the sheaf of bills on our breakfast table, held down by the ceramic butter dish, the bank notes ruffling in the breeze from the louvered windows that opened onto his green. In the note he said he had gone north and would call her when he'd settled. It was December. I told my mother that I would visit in a week, when school was out for Christmas. I told her to go to her sister's and stay there, and then I said that I was working and had to get back to my class. She didn't say anything on the other end of the line, and in the silence I imagined my father crisscrossing the state of California, driving north, stopping in Palm Springs and Carmel, the Lincoln riding low with the weight.

"Leonard," my mother said, "did you know anything like this was happening?"

During the spring of the year of getting to know us better I caddied for him a few times. On Saturdays he played early in the morning, when the course was mostly empty and the grass was still wet from the night. I learned to fetch the higher irons as the sun rose over the back nine and the ball, on drying ground, rolled farther. He hit skybound approach shots with backspin, chips that bit into the green and stopped. He played in a foursome with three other men, and in the locker room, as they changed their shoes, they told jokes and poked one another in the belly. The lockers were shiny green metal, the floor clean white tiles that clicked under the shoe spikes. Beneath the mirrors were jars of combs in green disinfectant. When I combed my hair with them it stayed in place and smelled like limes.

We were on the course at dawn. At the first fairway the other men dug in their spikes, shifted their weight from leg to leg, dummy-swung at an empty tee while my father lit a cigarette and looked out over the hole. "The big gun," he said to me, or, if it was a par three, "The lady." He stepped on his cigarette. I wiped the head with the club sock before I handed it to him. When he took the club, he felt its balance point, rested it on one finger, and then, in slow motion, he gripped the shaft. Left hand first, then right, the fingers wrapping pinkie to index. Then he leaned down over the ball. On a perfect drive the tee flew straight up in the air and landed in front of his feet.

Over the weekend his heart lost its rhythm for a few seconds. It happened Saturday night, when Anne and I were at the house in Sausalito, and we didn't hear about it until Sunday. "Ventricular fibrillation," the intern said. "Circus movements." The condition was always a danger after a heart attack. He had been given a shock and his heartbeat had returned to normal.

"But I'll be honest with you," the intern said. We were in the hall. He looked down, touched his stethoscope. "It isn't a good sign."

The heart gets bigger as it dies, he told me. Soon it spreads across the x-ray. He brought me with him to a room and showed me strips of paper with the electric tracings: certain formations. The muscle was dying in patches, he said. He said things might get better, they might not.

My mother called that afternoon. "Should I come up?"

"He was a bastard to you," I said.

When Lorraine and Anne were eating dinner, I found the intern again. "I want to know," I said. "Tell me the truth." The intern was tall and thin, sick-looking himself. So were the other doctors I had seen around the place. Everything in that hospital was pale—the walls, the coats, the skin.

He said, "What truth?"

I told him that I'd been reading about heart disease. I'd read about EKGs, knew about the medicines—lidocaine, propranolol. I knew that the lungs filled up with water, that heart failure was death by drowning. I said, "The truth about my father."

The afternoon I had hidden in the trunk, we came home while my mother was cooking dinner. I walked up the path from the garage behind my father, watching the pearls of sweat on his neck. He was whistling a tune. At the door he kissed my mother's cheek. He touched the small of her back. She was cooking vegetables, and the steam had fogged up the kitchen windows and dampened her hair. My father sat down in the chair by the window and opened the newspaper. I thought of the way the trunk rear had shifted when he and the woman had moved into the back of the Lincoln. My mother was smiling.

"Well?" she said.

"What's for dinner?" I asked.

"Well?" she said again.

"It's chicken," I said. "Isn't it?"

"Max, aren't you going to tell me if anything unusual happened today?"

My father didn't look up from the newspaper. "Did anything unusual happen today?" he said. He turned the page, folded it back smartly. "Why don't you ask Lenny?"

She smiled at me.

"I surprised him," I said. Then I turned and looked out the window.

"I have something to tell you," Anne said to me one Sunday morning in the fifth year of our marriage. We were lying in bed. I knew what was coming.

"I already know," I said.

"What do you already know?"

"I know about your lover."

She didn't say anything.

"It's all right," I said.

It was winter. The sky was gray, and although the sun had risen only a few hours earlier, it seemed like late afternoon. I waited for Anne to say something more. We were silent for several minutes. Then she said, "I wanted to hurt you." She got out of bed and began straightening out the bureau. She pulled my sweaters from the drawer and refolded them. She returned all our shoes to the closet. Then she came back to the bed, sat down, and began to cry. Her back was toward me. It shook with her gasps, and I put my hand out and touched her. "It's all right," I said.

"We only saw each other a few times," she answered. "I'd take it back if I could. I'd make it never happen."

"I know you would."

"For some reason I thought I couldn't really hurt you."

She had stopped crying. I looked out the window at the tree branches hung low with snow. It didn't seem I had to say anything.

"I don't know why I thought I couldn't hurt you," she said. "Of course I can hurt you."

"I forgive you."

Her back was still toward me. Outside, a few snowflakes drifted up in the air.

"*Did* I hurt you?"

"Yes, you did. I saw you two in a restaurant."

"Where?"

"At Denny's."

"No," she said. "I mean, where did I hurt you?"

The night he died, Anne stayed awake with me in bed. "Tell me about him," she said.

"What about?"

"Stories. Tell me what it was like growing up, things you did together."

"We didn't do that much," I said. "I caddied for him. He taught me things about golf."

That night I never went to sleep. Lorraine was at a friend's apartment and we were alone in my father's empty house, but we pulled out the sheets anyway, and the two wool blankets, and we lay on the fold-out sofa in the den. I told stories about my father until I couldn't think of any more, and then I talked about my mother until Anne fell asleep.

In the middle of the night I got up and went into the living room. Through the glass I could see lights across the water, the bridges, Belvedere and San Francisco, ships. It was clear outside, and when I walked out to the cement carport the sky was lit with stars. The breeze moved inside my nightclothes. Next to the garage the Lincoln stood half-lit in the porch floodlight. I opened the door and got in. The seats were red leather and smelled of limes and cigarettes. I rolled down the window and took the key from the glove compartment. I thought of writing a note for Anne, but didn't. Instead I coasted down the driveway in neutral and didn't close the door or turn on the lights until the bottom of the hill, or start the engine until I had swung around the corner, so that the house was out of sight and the brine smell of the marina was coming through the open windows of the car. The pistons were almost silent.

I felt urgent, though I had no route in mind. I ran one stop sign, then one red light, and when I reached the ramp onto Highway 101, I squeezed the accelerator and felt the surge of the fuel-injected, computer-sparked V-8. The dash lights glowed. I drove south and crossed over the Golden Gate Bridge at seventy miles an hour, its suspension cables swaying in the wind and the span rocking slowly, ocean to bay. The lanes were narrow. Reflectors zinged when the wheels strayed. If Anne woke, she might come out to the living room and then check for me outside. A light rain began to fall. Drops wet my knees, splattered my cheek. I kept the window open and turned on the radio; the car filled up with wind and music. Brass sounds. Trumpets. Sounds that filled my heart.

The Lincoln drove like a dream. South of San Francisco the road opened up, and in the gulley of a shallow hill I took it up over a hundred. The arrow nosed rightward in the dash. Shapes flattened out. "Dad," I said. The wind sounds changed pitch. I said, "The year of getting to know us." Signposts and power poles were flying by. Only a few cars were on the road, and most moved over before I arrived. In the mirror I could see the faces as I passed. I went through San Mateo, Pacifica, Redwood City, until, underneath a concrete overpass, the radio began pulling in static and I realized that I might die at this speed. I slowed down. At seventy drizzle wandered in the windows again. At fifty-five the scenery stopped moving. In Menlo Park I got off the freeway.

It was dark still, and off the interstate I found myself on a road without streetlights. It entered the center of town and then left again, curving up into shallow hills. The houses were large on either side. They were spaced far apart, three and four stories tall, with white shutters or ornament work that shone in the perimeter of the Lincoln's headlamps. The yards were large, dotted with eucalyptus and laurel. Here and there a light was on. Sometimes I saw faces: someone on an upstairs balcony; a man inside the breakfast room, awake at this hour, peering through the glass to see what car could be passing. I drove slowly, and when I came to a high school with its low buildings and long athletic field I pulled over and stopped.

The drizzle had become mist. I left the headlights on and got out and stood on the grass. I thought, This is the night your father has passed. I looked up at the lightening sky. I said it, "This is the night your father has passed," but I didn't feel what I thought I would. Just the wind on my throat, the chill of the morning. A pickup drove by and flashed its lights at me on the lawn. Then I went to the trunk of the Lincoln, because this was what my father would have done, and I got out the golf bag. It was heavier than I remembered, and the leather was stiff in the cool air. On the damp sod I set up:

dimpled white ball, yellow tee. My father would have swung, would have hit drives the length of the football field, high irons that disappeared into the gray sky, but as I stood there I didn't even take the clubs out of the bag. Instead I imagined his stance. I pictured the even weight, the deliberate grip, and after I had stood there for a few moments, I picked up the ball and tee, replaced them in the bag, and drove home to my wife.

The year I was sixteen we never made it to the American Southwest. My mother bought maps anyway, and planned our trip, talking to me about it at night in the dark, taking us in her mind across the Colorado River at the California border, where the water was opal green, into Arizona and along the stretch of desert highway to New Mexico. There, she said, the canyons were a mile deep. The road was lined with sagebrush and a type of cactus, jumping cholla, that launched its spines. Above the desert, where a man could die of dehydration in an afternoon and a morning, the peaks of the Rocky Mountains turned blue with sun and ice.

We didn't ever go. Every weekend my father played golf, and at last, in August, my parents agreed to a compromise. One Sunday morning, before I started the eleventh grade, we drove north in the Lincoln to a state park along the ocean. Above the shore the cliffs were planted with ice plant to resist erosion. Pelicans soared in the thermal currents. My mother had made chicken sandwiches, which we ate on the beach, and after lunch, while I looked at the crabs and swaying fronds in the tide pools, my parents walked to the base of the cliffs. I watched their progress on the shallow dunes. Once when I looked, my father was holding her in his arms and they were kissing.

She bent backward in his hands. I looked into the tide pool where, on the surface, the blue sky, the clouds, the reddish cliffs, were shining. Below them rock crabs scurried between submerged stones. The afternoon my father found me in the trunk, he introduced me to the woman in the back seat. Her name was Christine. She smelled of perfume. The gravel drive where we had parked was behind a warehouse, and after we shook hands through the open window of the car, she got out and went inside. It was low and long, and the metal door slammed behind her. On the drive home, wind blowing all around us in the car, my father and I didn't say much. I watched his hands on the steering wheel. They were big and red-knuckled, the hands of a butcher or a carpenter, and I tried to imagine them on the bend of Christine's back.

Later that afternoon on the beach, while my mother walked along the shore, my father and I climbed a steep trail up the cliffs. From above, where we stood in the carpet of ice plant, we could see the hue of the Pacific change to a more translucent blue—the drop-off and the outline of the shoal where the breakers rose. I tried to see what my father was seeing as he gazed out over the water. He picked up a rock and tossed it over the cliff. "You know," he said without looking at me, "you could be all right on the course." We approached the edge of the palisade, where the ice plant thinned into eroded cuts of sand. "Listen," he said. "We're here on this trip so we can get to know each other a little bit." A hundred yards below us waves broke on the rocks. He lowered his voice. "But I'm not sure about that. Anyway, you don't *have* to get to know me. You know why?"

"Why?" I asked.

"You don't have to get to know me," he said, "because one day you're going to grow up and then you're going to *be* me." He looked at me and then out over the water. "So what I'm going to do is teach you how to hit." He picked up a long stick and put it in my hand. Then he showed me the backswing. "You've got to know one thing to drive a golf ball," he told me, "and that's that the club is part of you." He stood behind me and showed me how to keep the left arm still. "The club is your hand," he said. "It's your bone. It's your whole arm and your skeleton and your heart." Below us on the beach I could see my mother walking the waterline. We took cut after cut, and he taught me to visualize the impact, to sense it. He told me to whittle down the point of energy so that the ball would fly. When I swung he held my head in position. "Don't just watch," he said. "*See.*" I looked. The ice plant was watery-looking and fat, and at the edge of my vision I could see the tips of my father's shoes. I was sixteen years old and waiting for the next thing he would tell me.

LIES

◆ ◆ ◆

WHAT MY FATHER SAID was, "You pays your dime, you takes your choice," which, if you don't understand it, boils down to him saying one thing to me: Get out. He had a right to say it, though. I had it coming and he's not a man who says excuse me and pardon me. He's a man who tells the truth. Some guys my age are kids, but I'm eighteen and getting married and that's a big difference. It's a tough thing to get squeezed from your own house, but my father's done all right because he's tough. He runs a steam press in Roxbury. When the deodorant commercials come on the set he turns the TV off. That's the way he is. There's no second chance with him. Anyway, I'll do all right. Getting out of the house is what I wanted, so it's no hair off my head. You can't get everything you want. This summer two things I wanted were to get out of the house finally and to go up to Fountain Lake with Katy, and I got both. You don't have that happen to you very often, so I'm not doing so bad.

It's summer and I'm out of High. That's a relief. Some guys don't make it through, but they're the ones I was talking about—the kids. Part of the reason I made it is that my folks pushed me. Until I was too old to believe it my mother used to tell me the lie that anybody can be what you want to. "Anybody can rise up to be President of the United States," she used to say. Somewhere along the line you find out that's not true and that you're either fixed from the start or fixed by something you do without really thinking about it. I guess I was fixed by both. My mother, though, she doesn't give up. She got up twenty minutes early to make me provolone on rye for four years solid and cried when I was handed my diploma.

After graduation is when I got the job at Able's. Able's is the movie theater—a two-hundred-fifty-seat, one-aisle house on South Huntington. *Able's, where the service is friendly and the popcorn is fresh.* The bathrooms are cold-water-only though, and Mr. Able spends Monday mornings sewing the ripped seat upholstery himself because he won't let loose a few grand to re-cover the loges, which for some reason are coming apart faster than the standard seats. I don't know why that is. I sell maybe one-third loge tickets and that clientele doesn't carry penknives to go at the fabric with. The ones who carry knives are the ones who hang out in front. They wouldn't cut anybody but they might take the sidewall off your tire. They're the ones who stopped at tenth grade, when the law says the state doesn't care anymore. They hang out in front, drinking usually, only they almost never actually come in to see the movie.

I work inside, half the time selling tickets and the other half as the projectionist. It's not a bad job. I memorize most movies. But one thing about a movie theater is that it's always dark inside, even in the lobby because of the tinted glass. (You've seen that, the way the light explodes in when someone opens the exit door.) But when you work in the ticket booth you're looking outside to where it's bright daylight, and you're looking through the metal bars, and sometimes that makes you think. On a hot afternoon when I see the wives coming indoors for the matinee, I want to push their money back under the slot. I want to ask them what in the world are they doing that for, trading away the light and the space outside for a seat here.

The projectionist half of the job isn't so bad, even though most people don't even know what one is. They don't realize some clown is sitting up in the room where the projectors are and changing the reels when it's time. Actually, most of the time the guy's just smoking, which he's not supposed to do, or he has a girl in there, which is what I did sometimes with Katy. All there is to do is watch for the yellow dot that comes on in the corner of the screen when it's time to change the reel. When I see that yellow dot there's five seconds before I have to have the other projector running. It's not hard, and after you do it a while you develop a sense. You get good enough so you can walk out to the lobby, maybe have popcorn or a medium drink, then sit on the stairs for a while before you go back to the booth, perfectly timed to catch the yellow spot and get the next reel going.

Anyway, it's pretty easy. But once I was in the booth with Katy when she told me something that made me forget to change the reel. The movie stopped and the theater was dark, and then everybody starts to boo and I hear Mr. Able's voice right up next to the wall. "Get on the ball, Jack," he says, and I have the other projector on before he even has time to open the door. If he knew Katy was in there he'd have canned me. Later he tells me it's my last warning.

What Katy told me was that she loved me. Nobody ever told me they loved me before except my mother, which is obvious, and I remember it exactly because suddenly I knew how old I was and how old I was getting. After she said that, getting older wasn't what I wanted so much. It's the way you feel after you get your first job. I remember exactly what she said. She said, "I love you, Jack. I thought about it and I know what I mean. I'm in love with you."

At the time the thing to do was kiss her, which I did. I wanted to tell her that I loved her too, but I couldn't say it. I don't mind lying, but not about that. Anyway, we're up there in the booth together, and it's while we have our tongues in each other's mouths that the reel runs out.

The first time I met Katy was at the theater. She's a pretty girl, all eyes, hair that's not quite blond. It falls a certain way. It was the thing I noticed first, the way it sat there on her shoulders. But it more than just sat; it touched her shoulders like a pair of hands, went in around the collar of her shirt and touched her neck. She was three rows in front. I wasn't working at the theater yet. It was end of senior year and I was sitting in two seats and had a box of popcorn in my lap. My friend LeFranc was next to me. We both saw Katy when she came in. LeFranc lit a match. "Put me out," he said, "before we all burn." LeFranc plays trumpet. He doesn't know what to say to a girl.

During the bright parts of the movie I keep looking at her neck. She's with three other girls we don't recognize. It turns out they go to Catholic school, which is why we don't know them. Then about halfway through she gets up by herself and heads back up the aisle. LeFranc breathes out and lights another match. I smile and think about following her back to the candy counter, where I might say something, but there's always the chance that she's gone out to the ladies' room instead and then where would I be? Time is on my side, so I decide to wait. The movie is *The Right Stuff.* They're taking up the supersonic planes when this is happening. They're talking about the envelope, and I don't know what that means, and then suddenly Katy's sitting next to me. I don't know where she came from. "Can I have some popcorn?" she says.

"You can have the whole box," I answer. I don't know

where this comes from either, but it's the perfect thing to say and I feel a little bit of my life happening. On the other side LeFranc is still as an Indian. I push the bucket toward Katy. Her hands are milk.

She takes a few pieces and holds them with her palm flat up. Already I'm thinking, That's something I would never do—the way she holds the little popped kernels like that. Then she chews them slowly, one by one, while I pretend to watch the movie. Things come into my head.

After the movie I talk to her a little and so we go on a few dates. In the meantime I get the theater job and in August she invites me to her sister's wedding. Her sister's marrying a guy twenty years older named Hank. It's at a big church in Saugus. By this time Katy and I've kissed maybe two hours total. She always bites a piece of Juicy Fruit in two when we're done and gives me half.

Anyway, at the wedding I walk in wearing a coat and tie and have to meet her parents. Her father's got something wrong with one of his eyes. I'm not sure which one's the bad one, and I'm worried he's thinking I'm shifty because I'm not sure which one to look at. We shake hands and he doesn't say anything. We put our hands down and he still doesn't say anything.

"I've been at work," I say. It's a line I've thought about.

"I don't know what the hell you kids want," he says then. That's exactly what he says. I look at him. I realize he's drunk or been drinking, and then in a second Katy's mother's all over him. At practically the same time she's also kissing me on the cheek and telling me I look good in my suit and pulling Katy over from where she's talking with a couple of her girlfriends.

For the ceremony we sit in the pews. I'm on the aisle, with her mother one row in front and a couple of seats over so that I can see all the pleats and hems and miniature flowers sewn into her dress. I can hear her breathing. The father, who's paid for the whole bagful, is pacing behind the nave door waiting to give away the bride. Katy's back there too, with the other maids. They're wearing these dresses that stay up without straps. The wedding starts and the maids come up the aisle finally, ahead of the bride, in those dresses that remind you all the time. Katy's at the front, and when they pass me, stepping slowly, she leans over and gives me half a piece of Juicy Fruit.

So anyway, we've already been to a wedding together and maybe thanks to that I'm not so scared of our own, which is coming up. It's going to be in November. A fall wedding. Though actually it's not going to be a wedding at all but just something done by a justice of the peace. It's better that way. I had enough the first time, seeing Katy's father pace. He had loose skin on his face and a tired look and I don't want that at our wedding.

And besides, things are changing. I'm not sure who I'd want to come to a big wedding. I'm eighteen in two months and so is Katy, and to tell the truth I'm starting to get tired of my friends. It's another phase I'm coming into, probably. My friends are Hadley and Mike and LeFranc. LeFranc is my best friend. Katy doesn't like Hadley or Mike and she thinks LeFranc is okay mostly because he was there when we met. But LeFranc plays amazing trumpet, and if there's a way for him to play at the justice-of-the-peace wedding I'm going to get him to do it. I want him to play because sometimes I think about how this bit with Katy started and how fast it's gone, and it kind of stuns me that this is what happened, that of all the ways a life can turn out this is the way mine is going to.

We didn't get up to Fountain Lake until a couple of months after her sister's wedding. It's a Sunday and I'm sitting on the red-and-black carpet of Able's lobby steps eating a medium popcorn and waiting for the reel change to come. Able himself is upstairs in the office, so I'm just sitting there, watching the sun outside through the ticket window, thinking this is the kind of day I'd rather be doing something else. The clowns out front have their shirts off. They're hanging around out there and I'm sitting in the lobby when a car honks and then honks again. I look over and I'm so surprised I think the sun's doing something to my eyes. It's Katy in a red Cadillac. It's got whitewalls and chrome and she's honking at me. I don't even know where she learned to drive. But she honks again and the guys out front start to laugh and point inside the theater. What's funny is that I know they can't see inside because of the tint, but they're pointing right at me anyway.

There's certain times in your life when you do things and then have to stick to them later, and nobody likes to do that. But this was one of them, and Katy was going to honk again if I didn't do something. My father has a saying about it being like getting caught between two rocks, but if you knew Mr. Able and you knew Katy, you'd know it wasn't really like two rocks. It was more like one rock, and then Katy sitting in a Cadillac. So I get up and set the popcorn down on the snack bar, then walk over and look through the door. I stand there maybe half a minute. All the while I'm counting off the time in my head until I've got to be back in to change the reel. I think of my father. He's worked everyday of his life. I think of Mr. Able, sewing on the loge upholstery with fishing line. They're banking on me, and I know it, and I start to feel kind of bad, but outside there's Katy in a red Fleetwood. "King of the Cadillac line," I say to myself. It's a blazing afternoon, and as soon as I open the door and step outside I know I'm not coming back.

On the street the sun's thrashing around off the fenders

and the white shirts, and it's like walking into a wall. But I cross the street without really knowing what I'm doing and get into the car on the driver's side. All the time I'm crossing the street I know everybody's looking, but nobody says anything. When I get into the car I slip the seat back a little.

"How'd you get this?"

"It's Hank's," she says. "It's new. Where should we go?"

I don't know what she's doing with Hank's car, but my foot's pushing up and down on the gas and the clowns out front are looking, so I have to do something and I say, "The lake, let's go up to Fountain Lake." I put it in drive and the tires squeal a second before we're gone.

The windows are up and I swear the car's so quiet I'm not sure there's an engine. I push the gas and don't hear anything but just feel the leather seats pushing up under our backs. The leather's cool and has this buttered look. The windshield is tinted at the top. After about three blocks I start thinking to myself, I'm out, and I wheel the Cadillac out Jamaicaway toward the river. I really don't know the way up to Fountain Lake. Katy doesn't either, though, so I don't ask her.

We cross over the river at BU and head up Memorial Drive, past all the college students on the lawns throwing Frisbees and plastic footballs. Over by Harvard they're pulling rowing sculls out of the water. They're all wearing their red jackets and holding big glasses of beer while they work. The grass is so green it hurts my eyes.

On the long stretch past Boylston I put down the electric window and hold my arm out so that the air picks it up like a wing when we speed up, and then, just before we get out to the highway, something clicks in my head and I know it's time to change the reel. I touch the brakes for a second. I count to five and imagine the theater going dark, then one of the wives in the audience saying something out loud, real irate. I see Mr. Able opening the door to the projection booth, the expression on his face just like one my father has. It's a certain look, half like he's hit somebody and half like somebody's hit him. But then as we come out onto Route 2 and I hit the gas hard one of my father's sayings comes to me, that it's all water over the bridge, and it's like inside my head another reel suddenly runs out. Just like that, that part of my life is gone.

By the time we're out past Lincoln I'm really not thinking anything except Wow, we're out of here. The car feels good. You get a feeling sometimes right after you do something. Katy's next to me with her real tight body and the soft way girls look, and I'm no kid anymore. I think about how nice it would be to be able to take the car whenever you want and go up to the lake. I'm thinking all this and floating the car around big wide turns, and I can see the hills now way up the road in front of us. I look over at Katy, and then at the long yellow line sliding under the front of the car, and it seems to me that I'm doing something big. All the time Katy's just sitting there. Then she says, "I can't believe it."

She's right. I'm on the way to Fountain Lake, going fast in a car, the red arrow shivering around seventy-five in the dial, a girl next to me, pretty, smelling the nice way girls do. And I turn to her and I don't know why except you get a feeling when you finally bust out, and I say, "I love you, Katy," in a certain kind of voice, my foot crushing the accelerator and the car booming along the straightaways like it's some kind of rocket.

WHERE
WE ARE NOW

◆ ◆ ◆

WHEN I MET JODI, she was an English major at Simmons College, in Boston, and for a while after that she tried to be a stage actress. Then she tried writing a play, and when that didn't work out she thought about opening a bookstore. We've been married eleven years now, and these days she checks out books at the public library. I don't mean she reads them; I mean she works at the circulation desk.

We've been arguing lately about where we live. Our apartment is in a building with no grass or bushes, only a social room, with plastic chairs and a carpet made of Astroturf. Not many people want to throw a party on Astroturf, Jodi says. She points out other things, too: the elevator stops a foot below the floors, so you have to step up to get out; the cold water comes out rusty in the mornings; three weeks ago a man was robbed in the hallway by a kid with a bread knife. The next Sunday night Jodi rolled over in bed, turned on the light, and said, "Charlie, let's look at houses."

It was one in the morning. From the fourth floor, through the night haze, I could see part of West Hollywood, a sliver of the observatory, lights from the mansions in the canyon.

"There," I said, pointing through the window. "Houses."

"No, let's look at houses to buy."

I covered my eyes with my arm. "Lovebird," I said, "where will we find a house we can afford?"

"We can start this weekend," she said.

That night after dinner she read aloud from the real estate section. "Santa Monica," she read. "Two bedrooms, yard, half-mile to beach."

"How much?"

She looked closer at the paper. "We can look other places."

She read to herself for a while. Then she said that prices seemed lower in some areas near the Los Angeles airport.

"How much?"

"A two-bedroom for $160,000."

I glanced at her.

"Just because we look doesn't mean we have to buy it," she said.

"There's a real estate agent involved."

"She won't mind."

"It's not honest," I said.

She closed the paper and went to the window. I watched a muscle in her neck move from side to side. "You know what it's like?" she said, looking into the street.

"I just don't want to waste the woman's time," I answered.

"It's like being married to a priest."

I knew why she said that. I'm nothing like a priest. I'm a physical education teacher in the Hollywood schools and an assistant coach—basketball and baseball. The other night I'd had a couple of other coaches over to the house. We aren't all that much alike—I'll read a biography on the weekend, listen to classical music maybe a third of the time—but I still like to have them over. We were sitting in the living room, drinking beer and talking about the future. One of the coaches has a two-year-old son at home. He didn't have a lot of money, he said, so he thought it was important to teach his kid morality. I wasn't sure he was serious, but when he finished I told a story anyway about an incident that had happened a few weeks before at school. I'd found out that a kid in a gym class I was teaching, a quiet boy and a decent student, had stolen a hat from a men's store. So I made him return it and write a letter of apology to the owner. When I told the part about how the man was so impressed with the letter that he offered the boy a job, Jodi remarked that I was lucky it hadn't turned out the other way.

"What do you mean?" I asked.

"He could have called the police," she said. "He could have thanked you for bringing the boy in and then called the police."

"I just don't think so."

"Why not? The boy could have ended up in jail."

"I just don't think so," I said. "I think most people will respond to honesty. I think that's where people like us have to lead the way."

It's an important point, I said, and took a drink of beer to take the edge off what I was saying. Too much money makes you lose sight of things, I told them. I stopped talking then, but I could have said more. All you have to do is look around: in Beverly Hills there's a restaurant where a piece of veal costs thirty dollars. I don't mind being an assistant coach at a high school, even though you hear now about the fellow who earns a hundred thousand dollars with the fitness truck that comes right to people's homes. The truck has Nautilus, and a sound system you wouldn't expect. He keeps the stars in shape that way—Kirk Douglas, the movie executives. The man with the truck doesn't live in Hollywood. He probably lives out at the beach, in Santa Monica or Malibu.

But Hollywood's fine if people don't compare it with the ideas they have. Once in a while, at a party, someone from out of town will ask me whether any children of movie stars are in my classes. Sometimes Jodi says the answer is yes but that it would violate confidentiality to reveal their names. Other times I explain that movie stars don't live in Hollywood these days, that most of them don't even work here, that Hollywood is just car washes and food joints, and that the theater with the stars' footprints out front isn't much of a theater anymore. The kids race hot rods by it on Thursday nights.

Hollywood is all right, though, I say. It's got sun and wide streets and is close to everything.

But Jodi wants to look anyway.

Next Sunday I drive, and Jodi gives directions from the map. The house is in El Segundo. While I'm parking I hear a loud noise, and a 747 flies right over our heads. I watch it come down over the freeway.

"Didn't one of them land on the road once?" I ask.

"I don't remember it," Jodi says. She looks at the map. "The house should be on this block."

"I think it was in Dallas. I think it came right down on top of a car."

I think about that for a minute. It shakes me up to see a huge plane so low. I think of the people inside the one that landed on the road—descending, watching the flaps and the ailerons, the houses and automobiles coming into view.

"The ad says there are nice trees in back," says Jodi.

She leads us to the house. It's two stories, yellow stucco walls, with a cement yard and a low wire fence along the sidewalk. The roof is tar paper. Down the front under the drainpipes are two long green stains.

"Don't worry," she says. "Just because we look doesn't mean anything." She knocks on the door and slips her arm into mine. "Maybe you can see the ocean from the bedroom windows."

She knocks again. Then she pushes the door a little, and we walk into the living room. There are quick footsteps, and a woman comes out of the hallway. "Good afternoon," she says. "Would you sign in, please?"

She points to a vinyl-covered book on the coffee table, and Jodi crosses the room and writes something in it. Then the agent hands me a sheet of paper with small type on it and a badly copied picture. I've never shopped for a house before. I see two columns of abbreviations, some numbers. It's hard to tell what the picture is of, but then I recognize the long stains under the drainpipes. I fold the sheet and put it into my pants pocket. Then I sit down on the couch and look around. The walls are light yellow, and one of them is covered with a mirror that has gold marbling in it. On the floor is a cream-colored shag rug, with a matted area near the front door where a couch or maybe a trunk once stood. Above the mantel is a painting of a blue whale.

"Do the appliances and plumbing work?" Jodi asks.

"Everything works," says the agent.

Jodi turns the ceiling light on and off. She opens and closes the door to a closet in the corner, and I glimpse a tricycle and a bag full of empty bottles. I wonder what the family does on a Sunday afternoon when buyers look at their house.

"The rooms have a nice feel," the agent says. "You know what I mean?"

"I'm not sure I do," I say.

"It's hard to explain," she says, "but you'll see."

"We understand," says Jodi.

In the marbled mirror I watch Jodi's reflection. Three windows look onto the front yard, and she unlatches and lifts each one.

"I like a careful buyer," says the agent.

"You can never be too thorough," Jodi answers. Then she adds, "We're just looking."

The agent smiles, drumming her fingers against her wrist. I know she's trying to develop a strategy. In college I learned about strategies. I worked for a while selling magazines over the phone: talk to the man if you think they want it; talk to the woman if you think they don't. I was thinking of playing ball then, semi-pro, and the magazine work was evenings. I was twenty-three years old. I thought I was just doing work until I was discovered.

"Why don't you two look around," I say now to the agent. "I'll stay here."

"Perfect," she says.

She leads Jodi into the next room. I hear a door open and shut, and then they begin talking about the floors, the walls, the ceiling. We aren't going to buy the house, and I don't like being here. When I hear the two of them walk out through the back door into the yard, I get up from the couch and go over to look at the painting above the mantel. It's an underwater view, looking below the whale as it swims toward the surface. Above, the sunny sky is broken by ripples. On the mantel is a little pile of plaster powder, and as I stand there, I realize that the painting has just recently been hung. I go back to the couch. Once on a trip up the coast I saw a whale that the tide had trapped in a lagoon. It was north of Los Angeles, along the coastal highway, in a cove sheltered by two piers of man-moved boulders. Cars were parked along the shoulder. People were setting up their cameras while the whale moved around in the lagoon, stirring up the bottom. I don't like to think about trapped animals, though, so instead I sit down and try to plan what to do tomorrow at practice. The season hasn't started yet, and we're still working on base-running—the double steal, leading from the inside of the bag. Baseball isn't a thing you think about, though; baseball *comes*. I'm an assistant coach and maybe could have been a minor league pitcher, but when I think of it I realize I know only seven or eight things about the whole game. We learn so slowly, I think.

I get up and go over to the painting again. I glance behind me. I put my head next to the wall, lift the frame a little bit, and when I look I see that behind it the plaster is stained brown from an interior leak. I take a deep breath and then put the frame back. From outside in the yard I hear the women speaking about basement storage space, and rather than listen I cross the room and enter a hallway. It smells of grease. On the wall, at waist level, are children's hand marks that go all the way to the far end. I walk down there and enter the kitchen. In it are a Formica table and four plastic chairs, everything made large by the low ceiling. I see a door in the corner, and when I cross the room and open it I'm surprised to find a stairway with brooms and mops hung above the banister. The incline is steep, and when I go up I find myself in the rear of an upstairs closet. Below me Jodi and the agent are still talking. I push through the clothes hanging in front of me and open the door.

I'm in the master bedroom now. A king-size bed stands in front of me, but something's funny about it, and when I look closer I think that it might be two single beds pushed together. It's covered by a spread. I stop for a moment to think. I don't think I'm doing anything wrong. We came here to see the house, and when people show their homes they take out everything of value so that they won't have to worry. I go to the window. Framing it is a new-looking lace curtain, pinched up in a tieback. I look out at a crab apple tree and some telephone wires and try to calculate where the ocean might be. The shadows point west, but the coastline is irregular in this area and juts in different directions. The view of the crab apple is pretty, spotted with shade and light—but then I see that in the corner behind the curtain the glass is splintered and has been taped. I lift the curtain and look at the pane. The crack spreads like a spider web. Then I walk back to the bed. I flatten my hands and slip them into the crevice between the two mattresses, and when I extend my arms the two halves come apart. I push the beds back together and sit down. Then I look into the corner, and my heart skips because I see that against the far wall, half-hidden by the open door, is an old woman in a chair.

"Excuse me," I say.

"That's all right," she says. She folds her hands. "The window cracked ten years ago."

"My wife and I are looking at the house."

"I know."

I walk to the window. "A nice view," I say, pretending to look at something in the yard. The woman doesn't say anything. I can hear water running in the pipes, some children outside. Tiny, pale apples hang among the leaves of the tree.

"You know," I say, "we're not really looking at the house to buy it."

I walk back to the bed. The skin on the woman's arms is mottled and hangs in folds. "We can't afford to buy it," I say. "I don't make enough money to buy a house and—I don't know why, but my wife wants to look at them anyway. She wants people to think we have enough money to buy a house."

The woman looks at me.

"It's crazy," I say, "but what are you going to do in that kind of situation?"

She clears her throat. "My son-in-law," she begins, "wants to sell the house so he can throw the money away." Her voice is slow, and I think she has no saliva in her mouth. "He has a friend who goes to South America and swallows everything, then comes back through customs with a plastic bag in his bowel."

She stops. I look at her. "He's selling the house to invest the money in drugs?"

"I'm glad you don't want to buy," she says.

I might have had a small career in baseball, but I've learned in the past eleven years to talk about other things. I was

twenty-three the last pitch I threw. The season was over and
Jodi was in the stands in a wool coat. I was about to get a
college degree in physical education. I knew how to splint a
broken bone and how to cut the grass on a golf green, and
then I decided that to turn your life around you had to start
from the inside. I had a coach in college who said he wasn't
trying to teach us to be pro ballplayers; he was trying to teach
us to be decent people.

When we got married, I told Jodi that no matter what
happened, no matter where things went, she could always
trust me. We'd been seeing each other for a year, and in that
time I'd been reading books. Not baseball books. Biogra-
phies: Martin Luther King, Gandhi. To play baseball right
you have to forget that you're a person; you're muscles, bone,
the need for sleep and food. So when you stop, you're saved
by someone else's ideas. This isn't true just for baseball players. It's true for anyone who's failed at what he loves.

A friend got me the coaching job in California, and as soon
as we were married we came west. Jodi still wanted to be an
actress. We rented a room in a house with six other people,
and she took classes in dance in the mornings and speech in
the afternoons. Los Angeles is full of actors. Sometimes at
parties we counted them. After a couple of years she started
writing a play, and until we moved into where we are now
we used to read pieces of it out loud to our six housemates.

By then I was already a little friendly with the people at
school, but when I was out of the house, even after two years
in Los Angeles, I was alone. People were worried about their
own lives. In college I'd spent almost all my time with another ballplayer, Mitchell Lighty, and I wasn't used to new
people. A couple of years after we graduated, Mitchell left to
play pro ball in Panama City, and he came out to Los Angeles
on his way there. The night before his plane left, he and I
went downtown to a bar on the top floor of a big hotel. We

sat by a window, and after a few drinks we went out onto the balcony. The air was cool. Plants grew along the edge, ivy was woven into the railing, and birds perched among the leaves. I was amazed to see the birds resting there thirty stories up on the side of the building. When I brushed the plants the birds took off into the air, and when I leaned over to watch them, I became dizzy with the distance to the sidewalk and with the small, rectangular shapes of the cars. The birds sailed in wide circles over the street and came back to the balcony. Then Mitchell put his drink on a chair, took both my hands, and stepped up onto the railing. He stood there on the metal crossbar, his wrists locked in my hands, leaning into the air.

"For God's sake," I whispered. He leaned farther out, pulling me toward the railing. A waiter appeared at the sliding door next to us. "Take it easy," I said. "Come on down." Mitchell let go of one of my hands, kicked up one leg, and swung out over the street. His black wingtip shoe swiveled on the railing. The birds had scattered, and now they were circling, chattering angrily as he rocked. I was holding on with my pitching arm. My legs were pressed against the iron bars, and just when I began to feel the lead, just when the muscles began to shake, Mitchell jumped back onto the balcony. The waiter came through the sliding door and grabbed him, but in the years after that—the years after Mitchell got married and decided to stay in Panama City—I thought of that incident as the important moment of my life.

I don't know why. I've struck out nine men in a row and pitched to half a dozen hitters who are in the majors now, but when I think back over my life, about what I've done, not much more than that stands out.

As we lie in bed that night, Jodi reads aloud from the real estate listings. She uses abbreviations: BR, AC, D/D. As she goes down the page—San Marino, Santa Ana, Santa Monica—I nod occasionally or make a comment.

When I wake up later, early in the morning, the newspaper is still next to her on the bed. I can see its pale edge in the moonlight. Sometimes I wake up like this, maybe from some sound in the night, and when I do, I like to lie with my eyes closed and feel the difference between the bed and the night air. I like to take stock of things. These are the moments when I'm most in love with my wife. She's next to me, and her face when she sleeps is untroubled. Women say now that they don't want to be protected, but when I watch her slow breathing, her parted lips, I think what a delicate thing a life is. I lean over and touch her mouth.

When I was in school I saw different girls, but since I've been married to Jodi I've been faithful. Except for once, a few years ago, I've almost never thought about someone else. I have a friend at school, Ed Ryan, a history teacher, who told me about the time he had an affair, and about how his marriage broke up right afterward. It wasn't a happy thing to see. She was a cocktail waitress at a bar a few blocks from school, he said. Ed told me the whole long story, about how he and the waitress had fallen in love so suddenly that he had no choice about leaving his wife. After the marriage was over, though, Ed gained fifteen or twenty pounds. One night, coming home from school, he hit a tree and wrecked his car. A few days later he came in early to work and found that all the windows in his classroom had been broken. At first I believed him when he said he thought his wife had done it, but that afternoon we were talking and I realized what had really happened.

We were in a lunch place. "You know," Ed said, "sometimes you think you know a person." He was looking into his glass. "You can sleep next to a woman, you can know the way she smiles when she's turned on, you can see in her hands when she wants to talk about something. Then you wake up one day and some signal's been exchanged—and you don't know what it is, but you think for the first time, *Maybe I don't know her.* Just something. You never know what the signal is." I looked at him then and realized that there was no cocktail waitress and that Ed had broken the windows.

I turn in bed now and look at Jodi. Then I slide the newspaper off the blanket. We know each other, I think. The time I came close to adultery was a few years ago, with a secretary at school, a temporary who worked afternoons. She was a dark girl, didn't say much, and she wore turquoise bracelets on both wrists. She kept finding reasons to come into my office, which I share with the two other coaches. It's three desks, a window, a chalkboard. One night I was there late, after everyone else had gone, and she came by to do something. It was already dark. We talked for a while, and then she took off one of her bracelets to show me. She said she wanted me to see how beautiful it was, how the turquoise changed color in dim light. She put it into my hand, and then I knew for sure what was going on. I looked at it for a long time, listening to the little sounds in the building, before I looked up.

"Charlie?" Jodi says now in the dark.

"Yes?"

"Would you do whatever I asked you to do?"

"What do you mean?"

"I mean, would you do anything in the world that I asked you to do?"

"That depends," I say.

"On what?"

"On what you asked. If you asked me to rob someone, then maybe I wouldn't."

I hear her roll over, and I know she's looking at me. "But don't you think I would have a good reason to ask you if I did?"

"Probably."

"And wouldn't you do it just because I asked?"

She turns away again and I try to think of an answer. We've already argued once today, while she was making dinner, but I don't want to lie to her. That's what we argued about earlier. She asked me what I thought of the house we looked at, and I told her the truth, that a house just wasn't important to me.

"Then what is important to you?"

I was putting the forks and knives on the table. "Leveling with other people is important to me," I answered. "And you're important to me." Then I said, "And whales."

"What?"

"Whales are important to me."

That was when it started. We didn't say much after that, so it wasn't an argument exactly. I don't know why I mentioned the whales. They're great animals, the biggest things on earth, but they're not important to me.

"What if it was something not so bad," she says now, "but still something you didn't want to do?"

"What?"

The moonlight is shining in her hair. "What if I asked you to do something that ordinarily you wouldn't do yourself—would you do it if I asked?"

"And it wasn't something so bad?"

"Right."

"Yes," I say. "Then I would do it."

"What I want you to do," she says on Wednesday, "is look at another house." We're eating dinner. "But I want them to take us seriously," she says. "I want to act as if we're really thinking of buying it, right on the verge. You know—maybe we will, maybe we won't."

I take a sip of water, look out the window. "That's ridiculous," I say. "Nobody walks in off the street and decides in an afternoon whether to buy a house."

"Maybe we've been looking at it from a distance for a long time," she says, "assessing things." She isn't eating her dinner. I cooked it, chicken, and it's steaming on her plate. "Maybe we've been waiting for the market to change."

"Why is it so important to you?"

"It just is. And you said you'd do it if it was important to me. Didn't you say that?"

"I had a conversation with the old woman in the yellow house."

"What?"

"When we looked at the other house," I say, "I went off by myself for a while. I talked with the old woman who was sitting upstairs."

"What did you say?"

"Do you remember her?"

"Yes."

"She told me that the owner was selling the house so he could use the money to smuggle drugs."

"So?"

"So," I say, "you have to be careful."

This Sunday Jodi drives. The day is bright and blue, with a breeze from the ocean, and along Santa Monica Boulevard the palm fronds are rustling. I'm in my suit. If Jodi talks to the agent about offers, I've decided I'll stay to the back, nod or shrug at questions. She parks the car on a side street and we walk around the corner and go into the lobby of one of the hotels. We sit down in cloth chairs near the entrance. A bellman carries over an ashtray on a stand and sets it between us; Jodi hands him a bill from her purse. I look at her. The bellman is the age of my father. He moves away fast, and I lean forward to get my shoulder loose in my suit. I'm not sure if the lobby chairs are only for guests, and I'm ready to

get up if someone asks. Then a woman comes in and Jodi
stands and introduces herself. "Charlie Gordon," I say when
the woman puts out her hand. She's in a gray pinstripe skirt
and a jacket with a white flower in the lapel. After she says
something to Jodi, she leads us outside to the parking circle,
where a car is brought around by the valet, a French car, and
Jodi and I get in back. The seats are leather.

"Is the weather always this nice?" Jodi asks. We pull out
onto Wilshire Boulevard.

"Almost always," the woman says. "That's another thing I
love about Los Angeles—the weather. Los Angeles has the
most perfect weather on earth."

We drive out toward the ocean, and as the woman moves
in and out of the lines of traffic, I look around the car. It's
well kept, maybe leased. No gum wrappers or old coffee cups
under the seat.

"Then you're looking for a second home?" the woman says.

"My husband's business makes it necessary for us to have a
home in Los Angeles."

I look at Jodi. She's sitting back in the seat, her hand
resting on the armrest.

"Most of the year, of course, we'll be in Dallas."

The street is curved and long with a grass island in the
middle and eucalyptus along its length, and each time the
car banks, I feel the nerves firing in my gut. I look at Jodi. I
look at her forehead. I look at the way her hair falls on her
neck, at her breasts, and I realize, the car shifting under us,
that I don't trust her.

We turn and head up a hill. The street twists, and we go
in and out of the shade from a bridge of elms. I can't see
anything behind the hedges.

"The neighborhood is lovely," the woman says. "We have a
twenty-four-hour security patrol, and the bushes hide everything from the street. We don't have sidewalks."

"No sidewalks?" I say.

"That discourages sightseeing," says Jodi.

We turn into a driveway. It heads down between two hedges to the far end, where a gravel half-circle has been cut around the trunk of a low, spreading fig tree. We stop, the agent opens Jodi's door, and we get out and stand there, looking at the house. It's a mansion.

The walls are white. There are clay tiles on the roof, sloped eaves, hanging vines. A narrow window runs straight up from the ground. Through it I can see a staircase and a chandelier. In college once, at the end of the season, the team had a party at a mansion like this one. It had windows everywhere, panes of glass as tall as flagpoles. The fellow who owned it had played ball for a while when he was young, and then gotten out and made big money. He was in something like hair care or combs then, and at the door each of us got a leather travel kit with our name embossed and some of his products inside. At the buffet table the oranges were cut so that the peels came off like the leather on a split baseball. He showed us through the house and then brought us into the yard. He told us that after all these years the game was still inside him. We stood on the lawn. It was landscaped with shrubs and willows, but he said he had bought the place because the yard was big enough for a four-hundred-foot straightaway center field.

Now the agent leads us up the porch stairs. She rings the bell and then opens the door; inside, the light is everywhere. It streams from the windows, shines on the wood, falls in slants from every height. There are oriental carpets on the floor, plants, a piano. The agent opens her portfolio and hands us each a beige piece of paper. It's textured like a wedding invitation, and at the top, above the figures, is an ink drawing of the house. The boughs of the fig tree frame the paper. I look down at it in my hand, the way I used to look down at a baseball.

The agent motions us into the living room. From there she leads us back through a glass-walled study, wisteria and bougainvillaea hanging from the ceiling, down a hallway into the kitchen. Through the windows spread the grounds of the estate. Now is the time, I think to myself, when I should explain everything.

"I think I'll go out back," Jodi says. "You two can look around in here."

"Certainly," the agent says.

After she leaves, I pretend to look through the kitchen. I open cabinets, run the water. The tap has a charcoal filter. The agent says things about the plumbing and the foundation; I nod and then walk back into the study. She follows me.

"I know you'll find the terms agreeable," she says.

"The terms."

"And one can't surpass the house, as one can see."

"You could fit a diamond in the yard."

She smiles a little bit.

"A baseball diamond," I say. I lean forward and examine the paned windows carefully. They are newly washed, clear as air. Among them hang the vines of bougainvillaea. "But some people look at houses for other reasons."

"Of course."

"I know of a fellow who's selling his house to buy drugs in South America."

She looks down, touches the flower in her jacket.

"People don't care about an honest living anymore," I say.

She smiles and looks up at me. "They don't," she says. "You're absolutely right. One sees that everywhere now. What line of work are you in, Mr. Gordon?"

I lean against the glassed wall. Outside, violet petals are spinning down beneath the jacarandas. "We're not really from Dallas," I say.

"Oh?"

Through the window I see Jodi come out onto the lawn around the corner of the house. The grass is beautiful. It's green and long like an outfield. Jodi steps up into the middle of it and raises her hands above her head, arches her back like a dancer. She was in a play the first time I ever saw her, stretching like that, onstage in a college auditorium. I was in the audience, wearing a baseball shirt. At intermission I went home and changed my clothes so that I could introduce myself. That was twelve years ago.

"No," I say to the agent. "We're not really from Dallas. We moved outside of Dallas a while back. We live in Highland Park now."

She nods.

"I'm an investor," I say.

WE ARE
NIGHTTIME
TRAVELERS

◆ ◆ ◆

WHERE ARE WE GOING? Where, I might write, is this path leading us? Francine is asleep and I am standing downstairs in the kitchen with the door closed and the light on and a stack of mostly blank paper on the counter in front of me. My dentures are in a glass by the sink. I clean them with a tablet that bubbles in the water, and although they were clean already I just cleaned them again because the bubbles are agreeable and I thought their effervescence might excite me to action. By action, I mean I thought they might excite me to write. But words fail me.

This is a love story. However, its roots are tangled and involve a good bit of my life, and when I recall my life my mood turns sour and I am reminded that no man makes truly proper use of his time. We are blind and small-minded. We are dumb as snails and as frightened, full of vanity and misinformed about the importance of things. I'm an average man, without great deeds except maybe one, and that has been to love my wife.

I have been more or less faithful to Francine since I married her. There has been one transgression—leaning up against a closet wall with a red-haired purchasing agent at a sales meeting once in Minneapolis twenty years ago; but she was buying auto upholstery and I was selling it and in the eyes of judgment this may bear a key weight. Since then, though, I have ambled on this narrow path of life bound to one woman. This is a triumph and a regret. In our current state of affairs it is a regret because in life a man is either on the uphill or on the downhill, and if he isn't procreating he is on the downhill. It is a steep downhill indeed. These days I am tumbling, falling headlong among the scrub oaks and boulders, tearing my knees and abrading all the bony parts of the body. I have given myself to gravity.

Francine and I are married now forty-six years, and I would be a bamboozler to say that I have loved her for any more than half of these. Let us say that for the last year I haven't; let us say this for the last ten, even. Time has made torments of our small differences and tolerance of our passions. This is our state of affairs. Now I stand by myself in our kitchen in the middle of the night; now I lead a secret life. We wake at different hours now, sleep in different corners of the bed. We like different foods and different music, keep our clothing in different drawers, and if it can be said that either of us has aspirations, I believe that they are to a different bliss. Also, she is healthy and I am ill. And as for conversation—that feast of reason, that flow of the soul—our house is silent as the bone yard.

Last week we did talk. "Frank," she said one evening at the table, "there is something I must tell you."

The New York game was on the radio, snow was falling outside, and the pot of tea she had brewed was steaming on the table between us. Her medicine and my medicine were in little paper cups at our places.

"Frank," she said, jiggling her cup, "what I must tell you is that someone was around the house last night."

I tilted my pills onto my hand. "Around the house?"

"Someone was at the window."

On my palm the pills were white, blue, beige, pink: Lasix, Diabinese, Slow-K, Lopressor. "What do you mean?"

She rolled her pills onto the tablecloth and fidgeted with them, made them into a line, then into a circle, then into a line again. I don't know her medicine so well. She's healthy, except for little things. "I mean," she said, "there was someone in the yard last night."

"How do you know?"

"Frank, will you really, please?"

"I'm asking how you know."

"I heard him," she said. She looked down. "I was sitting in the front room and I heard him outside the window."

"You heard him?"

"Yes."

"The front window?"

She got up and went to the sink. This is a trick of hers. At that distance I can't see her face.

"The front window is ten feet off the ground," I said.

"What I know is that there was a man out there last night, right outside the glass." She walked out of the kitchen.

"Let's check," I called after her. I walked into the living room, and when I got there she was looking out the window.

"What is it?"

She was peering out at an angle. All I could see was snow, blue-white.

"Footprints," she said.

I built the house we live in with my two hands. That was forty-nine years ago, when, in my foolishness and crude want of learning, everything I didn't know seemed like a promise. I learned to build a house and then I built one. There are copper fixtures on the pipes, sanded edges on the struts and queen posts. Now, a half-century later, the floors are flat as a billiard table but the man who laid them needs two hands to pick up a woodscrew. This is the diabetes. My feet are gone also. I look down at them and see two black shapes when I walk, things I can't feel. Black clubs. No connection with the ground. If I didn't look, I could go to sleep with my shoes on.

Life takes its toll, and soon the body gives up completely. But it gives up the parts first. This sugar in the blood: God says to me: "Frank Manlius—codger, man of prevarication and half-truth—I shall take your life from you, as from all men. But first—" But first! Clouds in the eyeball, a heart that makes noise, feet cold as uncooked roast. And Francine, beauty that she was—now I see not much more than the dark line of her brow and the intersections of her body: mouth and nose, neck and shoulders. Her smells have changed over the years so that I don't know what's her own anymore and what's powder.

We have two children, but they're gone now too, with children of their own. We have a house, some furniture, small savings to speak of. How Francine spends her day I don't know. This is the sad truth, my confession. I am gone past nightfall. She wakes early with me and is awake when I return, but beyond this I know almost nothing of her life.

I myself spend my days at the aquarium. I've told Francine something else, of course, that I'm part of a volunteer service of retired men, that we spend our days setting young businesses afoot: "Immigrants," I told her early on, "newcomers to the land." I said it was difficult work. In the evenings I could invent stories, but I don't, and Francine doesn't ask.

I am home by nine or ten. Ticket stubs from the aquarium fill my coat pocket. Most of the day I watch the big sea animals—porpoises, sharks, a manatee—turn their saltwater loops. I come late morning and move a chair up close. They are waiting to eat then. Their bodies skim the cool glass, full of strange magnifications. I think, if it is possible, that they are beginning to know me: this man—hunched at the shoulder, cataractic of eye, breathing through water himself—this man who sits and watches. I do not pity them. At lunchtime I buy coffee and sit in one of the hotel lobbies or in the cafeteria next door, and I read poems. Browning, Whitman, Eliot. This is my secret. It is night when I return home. Francine is at the table, four feet across from my seat, the width of two dropleaves. Our medicine is in cups. There have been three Presidents since I held her in my arms.

The cafeteria moves the men along, old or young, who come to get away from the cold. A half-hour for a cup, they let me sit. Then the manager is at my table. He is nothing but polite. I buy a pastry then, something small. He knows me—I have seen him nearly every day for months now—and by his slight limp I know he is a man of mercy. But business is business.

"What are you reading?" he asks me as he wipes the table with a wet cloth. He touches the saltshaker, nudges the napkins in their holder. I know what this means.

"I'll take a cranberry roll," I say. He flicks the cloth and turns back to the counter.

This is what:

Shall I say, I have gone at dusk through narrow streets
And watched the smoke that rises from the pipes
Of lonely men in shirt-sleeves, leaning out of windows?

Through the magnifier glass the words come forward, huge, two by two. With spectacles, everything is twice enlarged. Still, though, I am slow to read it. In a half-hour I am finished, could not read more, even if I bought another roll. The boy at the register greets me, smiles when I reach him. "What are you reading today?" he asks, counting out the change.

The books themselves are small and fit in the inside pockets of my coat. I put one in front of each breast, then walk back to see the fish some more. These are the fish I know: the gafftopsail pompano, sixgill shark, the starry flounder with its upturned eyes, queerly migrated. He rests half-submerged in sand. His scales are platey and flat-hued. Of everything upward he is wary, of the silvery seabass and the bluefin tuna that pass above him in the region of light and open water. For a life he lies on the bottom of the tank. I look at him. His eyes are dull. They are ugly and an aberration. Above us the bony fishes wheel at the tank's corners. I lean forward to the glass. *"Platichthys stellatus,"* I say to him. The caudal fin stirs. Sand moves and resettles, and I see the black and yellow stripes. "Flatfish," I whisper, "we are, you and I, observers of this life."

"A man on our lawn," I say a few nights later in bed.

"Not just that."

I breathe in, breathe out, look up at the ceiling. "What else?"

"When you were out last night he came back."

"He came back."

"Yes."

"What did he do?"

"Looked in at me."

Later, in the early night, when the lights of cars are still passing and the walked dogs still jingle their collar chains out front, I get up quickly from bed and step into the hall. I move fast because this is still possible in short bursts and with concentration. The bed sinks once, then rises. I am on the landing and then downstairs without Francine waking. I stay close to the staircase joists.

In the kitchen I take out my almost blank sheets and set them on the counter. I write standing up because I want to take more than an animal's pose. For me this is futile, but I stand anyway. The page will be blank when I finish. This I know. The dreams I compose are the dreams of others, re-membered bits of verse. Songs of greater men than I. In months I have written few more than a hundred words. The pages are stacked, sheets of different sizes.

If I could

one says.

It has never seemed

says another. I stand and shift them in and out. They are mostly blank, sheets from months of nights. But this doesn't bother me. What I have is patience.

Francine knows nothing of the poetry. She's a simple girl, toast and butter. I myself am hardly the man for it: forty years selling (anything—steel piping, heater elements, dried bananas). Didn't read a book except one on sales. Think vic-tory, the book said. Think *sale.* It's a young man's bag of apples, though; young men in pants that nip at the waist. Ten years ago I left the Buick in the company lot and walked home, dye in my hair, cotton rectangles in the shoulders of my coat. Francine was in the house that afternoon also, the way she is now. When I retired we bought a camper and went on a trip. A traveling salesman retires, so he goes on a trip. Forty miles out of town the folly appeared to me, big as a balloon. To Francine, too. "Frank," she said in the middle of a bend, a prophet turning to me, the camper pushing sixty and rocking in the wind, trucks to our left and right big as trains—"Frank," she said, "these roads must be familiar to you."

So we sold the camper at a loss and a man who'd spent forty years at highway speed looked around for something to do before he died. The first poem I read was in a book on a table in a waiting room. My eyeglasses made half-sense of things.

> *THESE*
> *are the desolate, dark weeks*

I read

> *when nature in its barrenness*
> *equals the stupidity of man.*

Gloom, I thought, and nothing more, but then I reread the words, and suddenly there I was, hunched and wheezing, bald as a trout, and tears were in my eye. I don't know where they came from.

In the morning an officer visits. He has muscles, mustache, skin red from the cold. He leans against the door frame.

"Can you describe him?" he says.

"It's always dark," says Francine.

"Anything about him?"

"I'm an old woman. I can see that he wears glasses."

"What kind of glasses?"

"Black."

"Dark glasses?"

"Black glasses."

"At a particular time?"

"Always when Frank is away."

"Your husband has never been here when he's come?"

"Never."

"I see." He looks at me. This look can mean several things, perhaps that he thinks Francine is imagining. "But never at a particular time?"

"No."

"Well," he says. Outside on the porch his partner is stamping his feet. "Well," he says again. "We'll have a look." He turns, replaces his cap, heads out to the snowy steps. The door closes. I hear him say something outside.

"Last night—" Francine says. She speaks in the dark. "Last night I heard him on the side of the house."

We are in bed. Outside, on the sill, snow has been building since morning.

"You heard the wind."

"Frank." She sits up, switches on the lamp, tilts her head toward the window. Through a ceiling and two walls I can hear the ticking of our kitchen clock.

"I heard him climbing," she says. She has wrapped her arms about her own waist. "He was on the house. I heard him. He went up the drainpipe." She shivers as she says this. "There was no wind. He went up the drainpipe and then I heard him on the porch roof."

"Houses make noise."

"I heard him. There's gravel there."

I imagine the sounds, amplified by hollow walls, rubber heels on timber. I don't say anything. There is an arm's length between us, cold sheet, a space uncrossed since I can remember.

"I have made the mistake in my life of not being interested in enough people," she says then. "If I'd been interested in more people, I wouldn't be alone now."

"Nobody's alone," I say.

"I mean that if I'd made more of an effort with people I

would have friends now. I would know the postman and the Giffords and the Kohlers, and we'd be together in this, all of us. We'd sit in each other's living rooms on rainy days and talk about the children. Instead we've kept to ourselves. Now I'm alone."

"You're not alone," I say.

"Yes, I am." She turns the light off and we are in the dark again. "You're alone, too."

My health has gotten worse. It's slow to set in at this age, not the violent shaking grip of death; instead—a slow leak, nothing more. A bicycle tire: rimless, thready, worn treadless already and now losing its fatness. A war of attrition. The tall camels of the spirit steering for the desert. One morning I realized I hadn't been warm in a year.

And there are other things that go, too. For instance, I recall with certainty that it was on the 23rd of April, 1945, that, despite German counteroffensives in the Ardennes, Eisenhower's men reached the Elbe; but I cannot remember whether I have visited the savings and loan this week. Also, I am unable to produce the name of my neighbor, though I greeted him yesterday in the street. And take, for example, this: I am at a loss to explain whole decades of my life. We have children and photographs, and there is an understanding between Francine and me that bears the weight of nothing less than half a century, but when I gather my memories they seem to fill no more than an hour. Where has my life gone?

It has gone partway to shoddy accumulations. In my wallet are credit cards, a license ten years expired, twenty-three dollars in cash. There is a photograph but it depresses me to look at it, and a poem, half-copied and folded into the billfold. The leather is pocked and has taken on the curve of my thigh. The poem is from Walt Whitman. I copy only what I need.

But of all things to do last, poetry is a barren choice. Deciphering other men's riddles while the world is full of procreation and war. A man should go out swinging an axe. Instead, I shall go out in a coffee shop.

But how can any man leave this world with honor? Despite anything he does, it grows corrupt around him. It fills with locks and sirens. A man walks into a store now and the microwaves announce his entry; when he leaves, they make electronic peeks into his coat pockets, his trousers. Who doesn't feel like a thief? I see a policeman now, any policeman, and I feel a fright. And the things I've done wrong in my life haven't been crimes. Crimes of the heart perhaps, but nothing against the state. My soul may turn black but I can wear white trousers at any meeting of men. Have I loved my wife? At one time, yes—in rages and torrents. I've been covered by the pimples of ecstasy and have rooted in the mud of despair; and I've lived for months, for whole years now, as mindless of Francine as a tree of its mosses.

And this is what kills us, this mindlessness. We sit across the tablecloth now with our medicines between us, little balls and oblongs. We sit, sit. This has become our view of each other, a tableboard apart. We sit.

"Again?" I say.

"Last night."

We are at the table. Francine is making a twisting motion with her fingers. She coughs, brushes her cheek with her forearm, stands suddenly so that the table bumps and my medicines move in the cup.

"Francine," I say.

The half-light of dawn is showing me things outside the window: silhouettes, our maple, the eaves of our neighbor's garage. Francine moves and stands against the glass, hugging her shoulders.

"You're not telling me something," I say.

She sits and makes her pills into a circle again, then into a line. Then she is crying.

I come around the table, but she gets up before I reach her and leaves the kitchen. I stand there. In a moment I hear a drawer open in the living room. She moves things around, then shuts it again. When she returns she sits at the other side of the table. "Sit down," she says. She puts two folded sheets of paper onto the table. "I wasn't hiding them," she says.

"What weren't you hiding?"

"These," she says. "He leaves them."

"He leaves them?"

"They say he loves me."

"Francine."

"They're inside the windows in the morning." She picks one up, unfolds it. Then she reads:

> *Ah, I remember well (and how can I*
> *But evermore remember well) when first*

She pauses, squint-eyed, working her lips. It is a pause of only faint understanding. Then she continues:

> *Our flame began, when scarce we knew what was*
> *The flame we felt.*

When she finishes she refolds the paper precisely. "That's it," she says. "That's one of them."

At the aquarium I sit, circled by glass and, behind it, the senseless eyes of fish. I have never written a word of my own poetry but can recite the verse of others. This is the culmination of a life. *Coryphaena hippurus,* says the plaque on the dolphin's tank, words more beautiful than any of my own. The dolphin circles, circles, approaches with alarming speed, but takes no notice of, if he even sees, my hands. I wave them in front of his tank. What must he think has become of the sea? He turns and his slippery proboscis nudges the glass. I am every part sore from life.

> *Ah, silver shrine, here will I take my rest*
> *After so many hours of toil and quest,*
> *A famished pilgrim—saved by miracle.*

There is nothing noble for either of us here, nothing between us, and no miracles. I am better off drinking coffee. Any fluid refills the blood. The counter boy knows me and later at the café he pours the cup, most of a dollar's worth. Refills are free but my heart hurts if I drink more than one. It hurts no different from a bone, bruised or cracked. This amazes me.

Francine is amazed by other things. She is mystified, thrown beam ends by the romance. She reads me the poems now at breakfast, one by one. I sit. I roll my pills. "Another came last night," she says, and I see her eyebrows rise. "Another this morning." She reads them as if every word is a surprise. Her tongue touches teeth, shows between lips. These lips are dry. She reads:

> *Kiss me as if you made believe*
> *You were not sure, this eve,*
> *How my face, your flower, had pursed*
> *Its petals up*

That night she shows me the windowsill, second story, rimmed with snow, where she finds the poems. We open the glass. We lean into the air. There is ice below us, sheets of it on the trellis, needles hanging from the drainwork.

"Where do you find them?"

"Outside," she says. "Folded, on the lip."

"In the morning?"

"Always in the morning."

"The police should know about this."

"What will they be able to do?"

I step away from the sill. She leans out again, surveying her lands, which are the yard's-width spit of crusted ice along our neighbor's chain link and the three maples out front, now lost their leaves. She peers as if she expects this man to appear. An icy wind comes inside. "Think," she says. "Think. He could come from anywhere."

One night in February, a month after this began, she asks me to stay awake and stand guard until the morning. It is almost spring. The earth has reappeared in patches. During the day, at the borders of yards and driveways, I see glimpses of brown—though I know I could be mistaken. I come home early that night, before dusk, and when darkness falls I move a chair by the window downstairs. I draw apart the outer curtain and raise the shade. Francine brings me a pot of tea. She turns out the light and pauses next to me, and as she does, her hand on the chair's backbrace, I am so struck by the proximity of elements—of the night, of the teapot's heat, of the sounds of water outside—that I consider speaking. I want to ask her what has become of us, what has made our breathed air so sorry now, and loveless. But the timing is wrong and in a moment she turns and climbs the stairs. I look out into the night. Later, I hear the closet shut, then our bed creak.

There is nothing to see outside, nothing to hear. This I know. I let hours pass. Behind the window I imagine fish moving down to greet me: broomtail grouper, surfperch, sturgeon with their prehistoric rows of scutes. It is almost possible to see them. The night is full of shapes and bits of light. In it the moon rises, losing the colors of the horizon, so that by early morning it is high and pale. Frost has made a ring around it.

A ringed moon above, and I am thinking back on things. What have I regretted in my life? Plenty of things, mistakes enough to fill the car showroom, then a good deal of the back lot. I've been a man of gains and losses. What gains? My marriage, certainly, though it has been no knee-buckling windfall but more like a split decision in the end, a stock risen a few points since bought. I've certainly enjoyed certain things about the world, too. These are things gone over and over again by the writers and probably enjoyed by everybody who ever lived. Most of them involve air. Early morning air, air after a rainstorm, air through a car window. Sometimes I think the cerebrum is wasted and all we really need is the lower brain, which I've been told is what makes the lungs breathe and the heart beat and what lets us smell pleasant things. What about the poetry? That's another split decision, maybe going the other way if I really made a tally. It's made me melancholy in old age, sad when if I'd stuck with motor homes and the national league standings I don't think I would have been rooting around in regret and doubt at this point. Nothing wrong with sadness, but this is not the real thing—not the death of a child but the feelings of a college student reading *Don Quixote* on a warm afternoon before going out to the lake.

Now, with Francine upstairs, I wait for a night prowler. He will not appear. This I know, but the window glass is ill-blown and makes moving shadows anyway, shapes that change in the wind's rattle. I look out and despite myself am afraid.

Before me, the night unrolls. Now the tree leaves turn yellow in moonshine. By two or three, Francine sleeps, but I get up anyway and change into my coat and hat. The books weigh against my chest. I don gloves, scarf, galoshes. Then I climb the stairs and go into our bedroom, where she is sleeping. On the far side of the bed I see her white hair and beneath the blankets the uneven heave of her chest. I watch the bedcovers rise. She is probably dreaming at this moment. Though we have shared this bed for most of a lifetime I cannot guess what her dreams are about. I step next to her and touch the sheets where they lie across her neck.

"Wake up," I whisper. I touch her cheek, and her eyes open. I know this though I cannot really see them, just the darkness of their sockets.

"Is he there?"

"No."

"Then what's the matter?"

"Nothing's the matter," I say. "But I'd like to go for a walk."

"You've been outside," she says. "You saw him, didn't you?"

"I've been at the window."

"Did you see him?"

"No. There's no one there."

"Then why do you want to walk?" In a moment she is sitting aside the bed, her feet in slippers. "We don't ever walk," she says.

I am warm in all my clothing. "I know we don't," I answer. I turn my arms out, open my hands toward her. "But I would like to. I would like to walk in air that is so new and cold."

She peers up at me. "I haven't been drinking," I say. I bend at the waist, and though my head spins, I lean forward enough so that the effect is of a bow. "Will you come with me?" I whisper. "Will you be queen of this crystal night?" I recover from my bow, and when I look up again she has risen from the bed, and in another moment she has dressed herself in her wool robe and is walking ahead of me to the stairs.

Outside, the ice is treacherous. Snow has begun to fall and our galoshes squeak and slide, but we stay on the plowed walkway long enough to leave our block and enter a part of the neighborhood where I have never been. Ice hangs from the lamps. We pass unfamiliar houses and unfamiliar trees, street signs I have never seen, and as we walk the night begins to change. It is becoming liquor. The snow is banked on either side of the walk, plowed into hillocks at the corners. My hands are warming from the exertion. They are the hands of a younger man now, someone else's fingers in my gloves. They tingle. We take ten minutes to cover a block but as we move through this neighborhood my ardor mounts. A car approaches and I wave, a boatman's salute, because here we are together on these rare and empty seas. We are nighttime travelers. He flashes his headlamps as he passes, and this fills me to the gullet with celebration and bravery. The night sings to us. I am Bluebeard now, Lindbergh, Genghis Khan.

No, I am not.

I am an old man. My blood is dark from hypoxia, my breaths singsong from disease. It is only the frozen night that is splendid. In it we walk, stepping slowly, bent forward. We take steps the length of table forks. Francine holds my elbow.

I have mean secrets and small dreams, no plans greater than where to buy groceries and what rhymes to read next, and by the time we reach our porch again my foolishness has subsided. My knees and elbows ache. They ache with a mortal ache, tired flesh, the cartilage gone sandy with time. I don't have the heart for dreams. We undress in the hallway, ice in the ends of our hair, our coats stiff from cold. Francine turns down the thermostat. Then we go upstairs and she gets into her side of the bed and I get into mine.

It is dark. We lie there for some time, and then, before dawn, I know she is asleep. It is cold in our bedroom. As I listen to her breathing I know my life is coming to an end. I cannot warm myself. What I would like to tell my wife is this:

> *What the*
> *imagination*
> *seizes*
> *as beauty must be truth. What holds you*
> *to what you see of me is*
> *that grasp alone.*

But I do not say anything. Instead I roll in the bed, reach across, and touch her, and because she is surprised she turns to me.

When I kiss her the lips are dry, cracking against mine, unfamiliar as the ocean floor. But then the lips give. They part. I am inside her mouth, and there, still, hidden from the world, as if ruin had forgotten a part, it is wet—Lord! I have the feeling of a miracle. Her tongue comes forward. I do not know myself then, what man I am, who I lie with in embrace. I can barely remember her beauty. She touches my chest and I bite lightly on her lip, spread moisture to her cheek and then kiss there. She makes something like a sigh. "Frank," she says. "Frank." We are lost now in seas and deserts. My hand finds her fingers and grips them, bone and tendon, fragile things.

PITCH MEMORY

◆ ◆ ◆

THE DAY AFTER Thanksgiving my mother was arrested outside the doors of J. C. Penney's, Los Angeles, and when I went to get her I considered leaving her at the security desk. I thought jail might be good for her.

I wasn't surprised—I'd known all along she was a thief. Small things: a bath towel if she stayed in a hotel, a couple of Red Delicious in her purse when she walked out of Safeway. "Why shouldn't I?" she said. "Who else is going to take care of us?" Since my father died eleven years ago in a lawn chair, she's been saying this to us. Since then there have been airplane tampons in our bathroom, hotel soaps in our tub. "No one's going to take care of you, either," she says to me now.

It's my first day home, two days before Thanksgiving, and already she has begun her warnings. "The world's an ugly place," she said at breakfast. "You've got to bait your own hooks." Now it is afternoon. "Susan B. Anthony," she calls to me out the kitchen window while I sweep the back yard walk. "Jane Austen."

"What are you saying, Mother?"

"I'm reading you my list of great women," she calls. "Emily Brontë. Maria Callas."

"What about *Charlotte* Brontë?" says my sister, Tessa.

My mother opens the window wider. "Charlotte was a lesser talent, honey." She smiles at Tessa. Tessa is a heart surgeon. "Marie Curie," says my mother.

"Don't forget Lizzie Borden," I say. I am a waitress.

Tessa and I are home because my mother thought it would be a good idea for all of us to spend Thanksgiving in our house in Pasadena. Tessa works in Houston and arranged to visit some conferences on the Coast in order to be here. I'm a print maker and a waitress in Burlington, Vermont, and came to California because there was a plane ticket and forty dollars for taxi fare in the envelope my mother sent me. I haven't been home in two years. My mother has called me almost weekly, sent me postcards asking when I planned to start my life. "The world won't wait for you," she said. "I can name other examples. Amelia Earhart, Beverly Sills—the world didn't have to wait for them." Over the phone she read me other lists: Virtues, Pitfalls, Courageous Decisions. She wrote me letters with the addresses of my father's old friends—lawyers and insurance brokers—and now and then these men have stopped on their business trips to telephone me from Vermont Holiday Inns.

"Your mother," said one, "is concerned about what you're doing with your life."

As soon as I stepped into my old room the first night, I knew she was stealing again. The box of Kleenex on my table said American Airlines; the vase on my dresser held a silk rose. I put down my bag and stepped into the bathroom, where I closed and locked the door. In the cabinet below the sink were stacks of paper towels, industrially wrapped, dozens of soap bars, sample size. I flushed the toilet, ran the tap, opened the door. My mother was standing there.

"Welcome home," she said.

"Thanks," I answered. "The house seems to be well stocked."

Her stealing started after my father died, though he had bought plenty of life insurance and had already made the last mortgage payment by the time his coronary artery closed up one Friday evening after work. That day became the meridian of my mother's life. For a year she wept at red lights and at drawers that didn't close. She began coaching my sister and me about the viciousness of the world, and she began feeding us a whole new kind of diet. She filled a cookie jar with vitamins, then distributed them every morning—a bloom of colors, a halo of pills that she set in a circle at our breakfast plates. It was a new series of associations. C, we learned, was for colds—or even cancer, according to the scientists she believed; E was for the elasticity of the skin, and D for the strength of our bones; B, we knew, was for the disposition— as if a pill would help—and for sleep, so my mother took it double dose. Still she had problems sleeping. For years I heard her go downstairs in the middle of the night. In the mornings her face was wax-yellow; her fingers tapped on the table top. Instead she dozed in the afternoons, in movie theaters or on the front room sofa, where the sunlight made her dreams bad, and she started stealing.

My father was a horn player when he was in the army, and on the bureau there are photos of him with trumpets, bugles, even a clarion. There he is in the photographs, a young man in uniform, and in the cellar of our house there are the instruments—maybe the same ones—hanging from a row of nails on a corkboard. My sister and I played them when we were in grammar school. As we were growing up our house was a litany of brass noises. My mother was a musician also, a pianist, and she taught my sister and me to play. Tessa could pick things up right off the radio, dance tunes that boys and then men tapped their feet to. When a new song came on the radio she leaned her ear right up against the grille of the speaker, and when the song was finished she went to the piano and played it, straight through, both hands. I don't know what she listened for when she put her ear so close to the radio. I tried it too, even tried going straight to the piano after and letting my fingers run over the keys without thought, imagining that was how Tessa did it. But whatever it was eluded me. Instead I practiced harder than my sister—major scales, minor scales, arpeggios, blues scales, chromatic scales. I could trill notes she barely had time to reach, but whatever she heard when she put her ear against the radio grille was as insensible to me as a dog whistle.

I started drawing instead. When I was a sophomore in high school I drew a picture of our piano, with a couple of my father's ancient horns resting on it, that was chosen for the school calendar. I drew the picture in October, and that December my father died. A few nights before it happened, a boy named Billy Emond had climbed the tree outside my window and come into my bedroom while my parents were downstairs watching television. I was fifteen and we had arranged this. He crawled through the window, took off his shirt in the dark room, and sat on the far end of my bed. He had one hand in his pocket and the other on the blankets around my feet when we heard my father on the stairs. My father loved to play tennis and took the stairs two and three in a leap. Billy had time to look at me, stand, and go into the corner of my room. My father came in. He said that the TV downstairs had gone fuzzy and that he thought the wind had knocked the antenna loose from outside my window. He said close my eyes, he was going to turn on the light. I closed my eyes. I heard the click of the light switch.

"Hello, Billy," said my father.

He didn't mention it the next day. That was a time when

I thought of my father as a person I would one day probably know. I remember coming into the kitchen on the evening after he died. My drawing, scissored from the school calendar, hung by banana magnets on the refrigerator.

Now, the first night we are all together, we sing. It is a tradition—voices only, no instruments. My mother hums a note, my sister comes in a third above it, and then they wait for me to find my note, which seems to lie between the pitches I can produce. We have always had this problem.

"Higher," says my mother.

I go higher with my note and then my mother and sister join me and suddenly the sounds are a chord as absolute as a piano's. "That's it," says Tessa.

My mother and sister harmonize in turn and I follow one of them in the melodies. They both have perfect pitch. My father had it also, but I do not. When he was alive the family played a game in which we identified cars by the pitches of their horns: we took mountain drives on the weekends, and as we went into the steep, blind turns beneath hoods of poplar and elm my father honked the horn of our Cutlass Supreme. That note, I knew, was a B-flat. If there was a car on the other side of the bend it honked too, and my mother and father and sister raced to identify it by pitch. I knew which notes came from which cars—the A of certain Pontiacs, our own B-flat, the sharp C of a Cadillac—but I didn't know the pitches when I heard them.

"Pontiac," I guessed sometimes.

"Of course not," said my mother.

"Way off," said Tessa.

My sister tried to teach me. She told me to reproduce the sound of our Cutlass horn in my head. "Then go up or down the scale from there," she said, "until you reach the note you've heard." I guessed at the cars, sometimes correctly, but I couldn't even reproduce our own B-flat. "Instead of perfect pitch," she said one day, "maybe it would help if you thought of it as something else. Think of it as pitch memory. You've heard all the notes before, so just try to remember them."

Sometimes in the morning she gave me a note. "Hum it," she said. "Hum it for me."

I hummed.

"Okay, now remember it all day."

I lost a certain part of my youth trying to remember notes. If the pitch was in my range I tried to speak in it all day. Otherwise, I kept it running in my skull.

"Okay," Tessa said at dinner, "now hum it for me."

I hummed.

"That's a C-sharp, honey," said my mother. "Your sister gave you an E."

Now, nineteen years later, on our first night together, in the living room of my mother's house, we sing. My mother is between us and we are facing the large plate-glass window that looks onto the bougainvillaea bushes and the sidewalk. It is just evening, and as we sing it grows darker outside so that the living room window starts to become a mirror. My mother notices this and puts a hand on each of our shoulders.

The next morning my mother and I drink tea in the kitchen. She wants to go clothes-shopping tomorrow and on the table she has arranged pages torn from fashion magazines. This year the models have short hair and the photographs are taken around urban fountains or in the marble entrance foyers of financial plazas. "Just choose anything you like," my mother says. "It doesn't mean a thing."

The shopping is her idea. Yesterday when I opened the covers of my bed there was an envelope on the sheets: inside, folded once, was a hundred-dollar bill.

"Mother," I called, "I have a job."

"What, honey?"

"I said I have a job already. A job. I earn money."

"I just thought you'd like to buy some clothes. You never know."

"What don't you ever know?"

"*You* know," she says.

That night I left the hundred-dollar bill on the kitchen table. My mother put it back on my bed. I hung it from the banana magnet on the refrigerator. She put it on my dresser. "Please," she said when I pinned it to the corkboard in the kitchen, "it's only to spruce you up a little." The next morning, talking to Tessa, I found it in my purse.

"Mom wants me to buy clothes," I said to Tessa.

"Maybe you should."

"I don't need clothes," I said. "I *have* clothes. I have two hundred skirts, maybe three hundred blouses."

"Be serious. She worries."

"She keeps trying to give me a hundred-dollar bill."

"Take it."

"I won't take it."

"The least you can do is let her buy you some clothes. You don't ever have to wear them. Put them on, get a picture taken, and send it to her. Then sell them."

"She's stealing again," I said.

"What?"

"Mom's stealing again."

"How do you know?"

"Look around. The bathroom closet's a supply warehouse."

"She worries about things running out."

"Why does she give me hundred-dollar bills, then?"

"She worries about you, too."

In the afternoon I clip the back yard grass while my mother watches from the kitchen. It is bright outside and I can see only her dark shape moving behind the window. When I finish, I rake the cuttings, then dump them in the plastic garbage pail in the garage. There are two cars in there still, my mother's Toyota and the big Cutlass, twenty years old now and still running because my mother wants a car for when her daughters come. Then I hand-snip the sidewalk borders and drag a chair to the northeast corner of the yard, where I know a triangle of sun persists until evening.

When I sit down she slides open the kitchen window and begins to read me a list of virtues. "Dedication," she says, "Discipline, Fortitude, Honor." It is not early and already the advancing shadows mark my calves.

In our family the violence has always been glancing and reflected. One Thanksgiving when my father was alive he dropped the platter he was carrying to the dining room, and the turkey, which my mother had been basting all afternoon, rolled onto the rug and under the table. "You might as well have dropped *me,*" said my mother, and the next day she backed out too close to the garage and tore the sideview mirror off my father's Cutlass.

Now it is Thanksgiving Day and my mother knows of an open store. It is run by immigrants, she tells me, who don't know the meaning of the holiday. We are in the car going to buy me some new clothes. The hundred-dollar bill lies on top of the dashboard, where I have placed it. My mother will not unlock the electric windows.

"I have a list for *you,*" I say to her. "Catherine Ablett, Melanie Green."

"Who are they?"

"They're from my high school class. Now they're street-walkers."

In the store she walks with her hand on her breast, not speaking, and in apology I finger the material of a few blouses, take a skirt into the dressing room. "Look," I tell her when we're outside again, "it's just that I don't need clothes. I'm happy, Mother. I don't want another job, I don't need a husband. I'm happy."

"Nothing's as secure as you think," she says. Then she takes the hundred-dollar bill from her purse. "Please," she whispers, "take the money. You don't have to spend it when I'm here. But please, will you take it?"

A group of men is watching us. She holds the bill out to me. "Will you take it?"

I do. I take it and place it, folded, in my purse.

For Thanksgiving dinner we go to a restaurant where the turkey is served in oval slices. We drink wine. My mother asks the waiter whether he minds working on Thanksgiving Day and he tells her that everybody's got to earn a living.

"That's right," my mother says when the waiter leaves.

"Mom, I *am* earning a living."

"Are you going to serve pancakes the rest of your life?"

"I think I will," I say, and this makes my mother start to cry. Tessa stands, goes to my mother's chair and helps her up, then walks her to the bathroom. There are a few other families in the restaurant and I'm sure they're looking at me. I sit alone at the table drinking my glass of wine. I wonder what my sister and mother are saying in the bathroom. I imagine the other diners in the restaurant getting up one by one, slinking away so I don't notice into the women's room, where my mother fills them in. *Yes,* my mother says and pauses, *the younger one—an artist. No,* says the man in the checked blazer, *not an artist. Yes, it's true,* says my mother, *and still not married.*

"You don't seem very sorry," Tessa says from behind me. She has returned alone.

"I'm not."

When my mother comes back to the table Tessa pours wine in all our glasses, makes a toast to some aspect of Thanksgiving. We eat. We talk about the smog in Pasadena and about how pleasant it is to get freshly baked rolls at a restaurant. My mother returns to the salad bar three times: her plate is a ruin of lettuce and onions.

The next afternoon, Tessa is at a conference discussing plastic heart valves and I am alone in the house when the phone rings and a man tells me that my mother has been detained for petty larceny outside the Los Angeles branch of J. C. Penney's. It is best if I come to the store.

So I do. I get the old Cutlass from the garage and drive to Penney's. The lot is full and I have to park on the street, and then, inside, I'm not sure how to ask where they are keeping a middle-aged woman whose Givenchy handbag brims with loot. I wait in line at the perfume counter. There are customers behind me, and I fumble with my purse, pretend I've forgotten something, and let them pass in front. I step back. A man asks if he can help and I tell him no. A group of Girl Scouts surrounds me, laughing in an ugly way, then passes down the aisle, and I move to the escalator, wondering where to proceed, before I think of looking at the store directory.

I find out the security desk is in the basement, and I take the escalator down. There, a man in something like a policeman's uniform tells me to come with him. His glasses are black mirrors. We pass through a door, down a hall, into a square yellow room where my mother is sitting at a table. She looks small.

The guard locks the door and offers me a chair. I sit down. "Well," he says.

On the table between my mother and me is a blouse.

"Well," he says again.

"A blouse," I say.

"Look," says my mother, "this is ridiculous."

"Ma'am, nothing at all like ridiculous." He looks at me.

"The article was in her handbag," he says, "and she was outside in the parking lot—on her way to the car, I'd say."

"You don't know that," says my mother.

He walks to a corner of the room, leans against the wall, lights a cigarette. He looks at us, then tucks his thumbs into his belt. "What are we going to do?" he says.

"This is ridiculous," says my mother, "arresting someone for forgetting to pay for a cheap blouse. At home my daughter has a closet of blouses that are twice as expensive."

"It was in your purse, ma'am."

"I was going to pay for it, obviously. Obviously I was going to pay for it. Look—ask my daughter. Don't I often forget? Ask her. Don't I often forget, honey?"

The guard looks at me.

"You did have it outside the store," I say.

My mother will not look at me and I will not look at her. In the guard's black sunglasses the room is reflected. Then I imagine my mother in her neat skirt in front of a magistrate. I imagine her arraignment, some sort of trial or perhaps the decision of a judge only, a man her age. He'll send her—for a day or two, perhaps a week or a month—to one of the low-security prisons in the valley north of here. I have seen one of them from the road: low, sand-colored, circled by a metal fence, it stands behind a row of cypress and a rectangular highway sign.

"I'm going to call the police now," the guard says and picks up the telephone—and it is only then, when I do it, that it seems obvious. The guard holds the phone away from him, looks down at my hand half-covered by my purse. He looks at the floor, then at my hand again.

"Who else knows?" I ask.

"Just me," he says. He looks down. He rubs his chin. Then his arm moves and the bill is out of my fingers and into the pocket of his shirt.

* * *

On the way home my mother drives her own car and I drive the old Cutlass. At red lights we look at each other through the windows. The day, somehow past, is already darkening, and when we arrive the house is empty. My mother goes into the kitchen and I go into the television room, where I turn on a movie and sit on the couch. I have entered too late to understand. Soldiers have arrived somewhere to save something, although they don't look like soldiers and I'm not sure who is on which side. The music is full of clock-ticking rhythms. After a while my mother comes in. She could sit in the wood desk chair or my father's old lazy lounger, but instead she places herself next to me on the couch, leaning against my shoulder. On my arm I feel where the sweat has wet her blouse.

We watch the movie for a while before I realize she is asleep. Her breathing becomes slow. She leans heavily against my shoulder, her head tilted back, and as we sit there her weight begins to make my forearm tingle. Tessa once explained this tingling to me: it is not the blood circulation being cut off, but a disturbance of the nerves. The funny throbbing spreads to my elbow, and my mother opens her mouth, and, though she still seems to be asleep, she begins to quietly hum. I sit still.

Presently I hear Tessa come into the house. The door thuds, the coat rack jingles. I put my finger to my lips, and when she peeks into the TV room I motion for her to stay quiet. She comes in and leans down next to us to listen. Then she goes over and turns off the TV. My mother's humming pauses, then continues, and Tessa goes out to the kitchen, where I hear her begin to cook our dinner. Pots clang on the stove, silverware chimes on the wood table. I lie still. My mother's humming is soft, almost inaudible. Despite all science, I think, we will never understand the sadness of certain notes.

AMERICAN
BEAUTY

◆ ◆ ◆

WHEN MY BROTHER Lawrence left us to live in California I should have tried to stop him, but I didn't, and I should have been sad, but I wasn't. Instead it was just something happening in our lives. It was like the roof leaking or the electricity going out. I thought of him riding the Trailways bus across the western states, underneath the bubble skylight, sharing cigarettes in station diners, talking with girls he didn't know. I thought of his new life in the Electronics Belt. I imagined going out to see him in a couple of years, heading out to California to stay with him in a split-level ranch with a dark-bottom pool. He was twenty-seven and I was sixteen and computers were booming.

On the morning he left, my mother gave him a Bible. I gave him a watch with a built-in compass, and our sister, Darienne, who was nineteen, gave him a four-by-six-foot oil portrait of our family, framed.

"I'm going to have to take it out of the frame," Lawrence said.

"But it's of our family."

"Dary, I'm taking a bus." Lawrence looked at me.

"Dary," I said, "he'll break down the frame and roll up the canvas. It's done all the time."

"I worked six weeks on it," she said. She started to cry.

"Don't worry," I said. "He'll be back soon."

Lawrence held up the painting. In it we were sitting to-gether in our kitchen—my brother, my sister, my mother, our spaniel named Caramel, and I. Lawrence's wrist dipped below the back of Darienne's collarbone so that his bad hand was hidden around her shoulder.

My father was in the painting also, or at least Darienne's idea of him. He had left fourteen years ago, and not even Lawrence remembered much about him. We certainly never talked about him anymore. But Darienne still put him into her paintings. In them he had a hooked nose, a straight nose, the faintly Indian nose and angled cheekbones that I think he really did have; he had thinning hair, full hair; he stared out from the canvases, scowled out, held his head turned away from us. He had been a civil engineer. He had stolen some money from his company and left with a woman who was one of my mother's good friends. One of the few times my mother spoke of him after that, years later, she told me that he was looking for something he would never find. In the painting Darienne now gave Lawrence he stood behind my mother. His arm rested on Darienne's shoulder, and he was smiling. He almost never smiled in Darienne's paintings.

"He's smiling," I said.

"He knows Lawrence is going to stay."

"I'm not staying, Dary."

"He's not staying," I said.

"He knows he's coming back soon, then," she said.

Lawrence was leaving because things had reached a point for him here. Although my mother said the good Lord sub-tracted five years from his age, the five years he spent fighting in blacktop lots and driving a car with no hood over the engine, twenty-seven was still old for him to be living where he was, in the basement of our house. He had an engineering degree from Hill Oak College and a night certificate in com-puter programming. His job, teaching math and auto mechanics at the high school, had ended in June, and on top of that my sister was having a bad summer. In July she had shown me a little black capsule inside the case where she kept her oboe reeds. We were alone in her room.

"Do you know what it is?"

"Cold medicine," I answered.

"Nope," she said. She put it on her tongue and closed her mouth. "It's cyanide."

"No, it's not."

"It is so."

"Dary, take that out of your mouth." I put my hand on her jaw, tried to get my finger between her lips.

"I'm not Caramel."

"Caramel wouldn't eat cyanide." I could feel the tips of her incisors nibbling my fingers. Finally I got my hand into her mouth.

"It's not cyanide," she said. "And get your hands out of my mouth." I pulled the pill out and held it on my palm. Saliva was on my fingers.

"You're crazy," I said to her. Then I regretted it. I wasn't supposed to say that to her. My mother had taken me aside a few years before and told me that even though my sister and I had lived together all our lives, I might still never under-stand her. "It's difficult for her to be around all you men," my mother said to me. "You and Lawrence are together somehow, and that's a lot for your sister." Then she told me never to call Darienne crazy. She said this was important, something I should never forget. I was thirteen or fourteen years old. "Whatever you do," she said, tilting her head forward and looking into my eyes, "whatever happens, I want you to re-member that."

At the beginning of the summer, before I knew he was leav-ing, Lawrence said he had something very important to tell me. "But I'm not just going to tell you," he said. "I'll mix it

into the conversation. I'll say it some time over the summer."
We were working on my motorcycle, which he had given me.
"You have to figure out what it is," he said. He had drilled
the rusted bolts on the cam covers and we were pulling them
out. "It's about time you started doing that anyway."

"Doing what?"

"Thinking about what's important."

We were living in Point Bluff, Iowa, in the two-story,
back-porched saltbox my father had bought before he left us.
As we took apart the rusting cams I tried to decide what was
important in our lives. Nothing had changed since I could
remember. Lawrence still lived in the basement, where at
night the green light of his computer filled the window. Darienne was using the summer to paint still lifes and practice
the Bellini oboe concerto, and I was going to go to baseball
day camp in August. My mother sipped vodka cranberries
out on the lawn furniture with Mrs. Silver in the evenings,
and at night sat on the porch reading the newspaper or sometimes the Bible and watching the *Tonight* show. She was the
high school guidance counselor and she believed the Lord had
a soft spot for the dropouts and delinquents she had to talk
with every day. Mrs. Silver was her best friend. Mrs. Silver
was young, maybe ten years younger than my mother, and
read the Bible, too, although she liked the newspaper more.
My mother said she'd led a rough life. She didn't look that
way to me, though. To me, my mother looked more like the
one with the rough life. Sometimes she wore a bathrobe all
weekend, for example. I didn't know any other mothers who
did that. And except for the two or three times a week when
she cooked, Lawrence and Darienne and I made our own dinners. My mother's arms were pale and her elbows were red.
Mrs. Silver's were tan. Mrs. Silver wore three or four bracelets, a gold chain on her ankle, and blouses without sleeves.
She came over almost every day. I talked to her sometimes in
the back yard when my mother went inside to answer the

phone or mix another pitcher of vodka cranberry. Mostly we talked about my future.

"It's not too early to think about college," she told me.

"I know, Mrs. Silver."

"And you ought to be saving money." She put her hands on her hips. "Are you saving money?"

"No."

"Do you know that life can be cruel?" she asked.

"Yes."

"No you don't," she said. She laughed. "You don't really know that."

"Maybe I don't."

"Are you learning, at least?"

"Yes," I answered. "I'm trying to decide what's important." I nodded. "Right now I'm learning about motorcycles."

Lawrence and I were taking apart the Honda CB 360 he had given me. We planned to have it completely rebuilt before baseball camp. He had given it to me in March, when the weather warmed and the melting snow uncovered it in the ditch by Route 80. It was green. The front fork had been bent double from impact, and when I touched the rusted chain it crumbled in my hands.

The first thing we took apart was the clutch. We loosened the striker panel and let the smooth round plates, bathed in oil, spill one by one into an aluminum turkey-roasting pan. With the oil wiped clean, they gleamed like a metal I had never seen before, the way I imagined platinum gleamed. They were polished from their own movement. Lawrence explained that the slotted panels were to dissipate heat from friction. After we took the plates out and examined them, noted how they slipped smoothly over their fellows, we put them back in. "That's how you learn a machine," he said. "You take it apart and then you put it back together."

I thought about this for a moment. "Is that what you were going to tell me?"

"No, Edgar," he said. "That's not important enough."

That spring, before he gave me the motorcycle, he had taught me his theory of machinery. In April he took me out to the back yard, to a patch of the softening earth that he had cleared of the elephant grass that grew everywhere else on the lot. He had sunk four poles there and made a shanty with fluted aluminum, sloping the ground so that snowmelt poured into two gulleys and flowed away from the center, where his machinery lay. His machinery was anything he could get his hands on. He got it from junkyards and road gulleys and farm sales. He made sealed bids on government surplus, brought home sump pumps, rifle mechanisms, an airplane engine, hauled them in a borrowed truck and set them underneath the shanty to be taken apart.

"Every machine is the same, Edgar," he told me one evening. "If you can understand two sticks hitting together, you can understand the engine of an airplane." We were standing underneath the shanty with Darienne and Mrs. Silver, who had wandered out to the back yard after dinner. Out there Lawrence kept a boulder and a block of wood and a walking stick to demonstrate the lever. "I can move the boulder with the stick," he said that evening, and then he did it. He wedged the stick between the wood and the rock, and when he leaned on it the boulder rolled over. "Fulcrum—lever—machine," he said. "Now"—and then he took the oilcloth tarp off the drag-racer engine and the Cessna propellor—"this is the very same thing."

"Spare me," said Darienne.

"If you don't want to learn," said Lawrence, "don't come out here."

Then my sister walked back across the yard, stopping to pick up a cottonweed pod for one of her still lifes. Lawrence watched her go in through the screen door. "She's crazy," he said.

I turned to him. "It's hard for her to be around all us men."

Mrs. Silver looked at me. "Good, Edgar," she said.

I smiled.

My brother picked up a wrench. He cleared his throat. "That's peckerdust," he said.

"Pardon me," said Mrs. Silver.

"I said that's peckerdust. Darienne can take what I give her. People like it when you're hard on them." He looked at her. "Everybody knows that. And you know what?" He transferred the wrench to his bad hand and pushed back his hair. "They come back for more."

"A lady wouldn't come back for more," said Mrs. Silver. She put her hands together in front of her. "And a gentleman wouldn't say that."

Lawrence laughed. "Well, Dary sure likes it. And she comes back."

"It's a nice night out here," I said.

Mrs. Silver smiled at me. "It is," she said. Then she turned and walked back to the house. The kitchen light went on. I saw Darienne at the sink putting water on her face. I watched her wipe the water from her eyes with a paper towel and then move away from the window.

Sometimes I tried to look at my sister as if she were a stranger. We spent a lot of time in the house together, she and my mother and I, and I had a lot of time to look at her. She was tall, with half-curly, half-straight hair and big shoulders. Sometimes Mrs. Silver sat with us. Mrs. Silver was lonely, my mother said. She had a husband who drank. She was beautiful, though. "I'm your mother's charity case," she would say, sitting in our yard chair while she and my mother waxed each other's legs. "Your mother just feels sorry for me." Sometimes I compared her with my sister. I watched her in the yard or on the other side of the family room as she smiled and laughed, as she brushed her bangs from her forehead or drank a vodka cranberry from a straw. Then I looked at Darienne. While she painted or played oboe, as if I were seeing her for the first time at a dance, I watched her. Her hands moved. She had the potential to be pretty but she wasn't. This is what I decided. Not the way she was now, at least. Her face was friendly, but she wore boy's cotton shirts and slumped her shoulders. In her shirt pocket she kept oboe reeds, which she always sucked.

"You ought to stand up straight," Lawrence told her.

"So I can be prettier for you? I'd rather die."

"No you wouldn't," said my mother.

"And you shouldn't suck those things in public," said Lawrence.

Darienne closed her lips tight. Whenever Lawrence corrected her, she pursed them so that they turned almost white. I thought this had something to do with her epilepsy, which she'd had since childhood, but I wasn't sure. She had been a special needs student in high school. Although we were never allowed to see her report card, I think she flunked most subjects. It wasn't because she was unintelligent, my mother said to Lawrence and me, but because there was a different force driving her. She painted beautifully, for example—"like a professional," said my mother—and played second oboe in school orchestra. But something about the epilepsy, I guess, made her slow. My mother parceled out her medicine in small plastic bottles that Darienne kept on her dresser. She never had any fits—she only had the *petit mal* disease—but she slept with cloth animals in her bed at age nineteen and used a Bambi nightlight. It was small and plastic and shaped like a deer.

Although Lawrence never paid much attention to her, Darienne still liked to show him everything she made and everything she found. At the end of most days she went downstairs to the basement with sheets of her sketch paper in her hand. She stayed in his apartment for a few minutes, then came back up.

"Why do you just draw lines?" I said to her one afternoon when she came upstairs.

"I don't. I draw plenty of things."

"I've seen you just drawing lines." I grabbed her hand. "Let me see."

"Edgar, you don't care what I draw."

"I *don't* care," I said. "You're right. I just want to see."

Really, though, I did care. I wasn't sure whether I cared about her because she was my sister, or just because there was something wrong with her, but I did care. She didn't think I did, though. For my birthday that year she had given me a diary, and inside, on the flyleaf, she had written in ornate calligraphy: *I DON'T THINK YOU CARE ABOUT ANY-THING*. And below that, in small letters: (BUT IF YOU DO, WRITE IT IN HERE). Underneath that, she had made a sketch of the sculpture *The Thinker*. It was a good sketch, and in parentheses even lower on the page, in even smaller writing, she wrote, AUGUST RODIN.

Darienne was a good artist. In the mornings she did drawing exercises. She sat in the window bay of her bedroom, our yard and the drainage canal curving below her, the hills with their elephant grass and vanilla pines in the distance, and she drew lines. She wouldn't show me, but I saw them anyway when I was in her room. They were curved, straight, varied in thickness, drawn with the flat edge or the sharp point of the pencil.

"That's a nice one, Dary," I said one morning as I passed behind her while she was drawing at the window. "Where did you get the idea for that one?"

That afternoon she came out to the yard where Lawrence and I were pulling out tiny screws and springs from the motorcycle carburetor. "You know, Edgar," she said, "all great artists practice their lines."

"Actors practice their lines," I said.

Lawrence laughed.

She pressed her lips together. "*You* know what I mean," she said. She walked around until her shadow fell on the carburetor. Then she stood there. "Maybe now," she said, "you two want to go out and shoot some animals."

"You're weird, Dary," said Lawrence.

"I'm not weird. You guys are weird." She threw a dirt clod in our oil pan. "Not everyone feels the same forces."

"You going to clean that dirt out?" said Lawrence.

"Why? So you can spend eight more hours taking out a cylinder?"

"We're working on the carburetor," I said.

"It looks like Lawrence is doing everything."

I loosened a small mixture screw. "If I practiced the oboe as much as you," I said, "I'd be Doc Severinsen."

She worked her lips. "Doc Severinsen plays the trumpet."

"He plays the oboe, too." I looked at Lawrence. I had made this up.

"The oboe is a double reed," Dary said. "It's one of the most difficult instruments."

The truth was, she was right. I had heard that the oboe was a fairly difficult instrument, and Darienne was pretty good on it. She could have played first oboe in school orchestra, but she played second because Mr. MacFarquhar, the director, didn't want her to have the responsibility. I felt bad saying the things I said to her. But she brought them on herself. I would have had conversations with her, but they never worked out.

"I hope the dirt clogs your engine," she said.

Lawrence made up a game that year that Darienne hated and that we played on all our car trips. It was called What Are You Going to Do? Lawrence drove and led the game. "You are driving along the summit pass of a mountain," Lawrence said one evening as he drove, "when under your foot you notice that the accelerator has become jammed in the full open position. You are approaching dangerous curves and the car is accelerating rapidly." He rolled down his window, propped his elbow out, adjusted the mirror to give us time to think. My mother shifted in her seat. "What are you going to do?" he asked.

"Press the brakes," said my mother.

"You'll burn them out." He adjusted his headrest.

"Steer like hell," said Mrs. Silver. Lawrence smiled.

"Open the door and roll out onto the road," said Darienne.

"You'll kill other drivers and possibly yourself." He put the blinker on and passed another car. "Edgar?"

"Shift the transmission into neutral," I answered.

"Bingo," he said. He leaned back and began whistling.

In high school, Lawrence had been in one piece of trouble after the next. He had broken windows and stolen cars and hit someone once, or so one of my teachers later told me, with a baseball bat. I knew about a lot of it because the school faculty told me. "You're Lawrence's brother," the older ones always said to me, more than a decade later, at the start of a new school year. Then they told the story about him stealing all the school's lawnmowers or driving a car into the Mississippi River. I never asked Lawrence about the bat because I couldn't imagine my brother doing that to anyone. I did ask him about some of the other things, though. He had broken into a gas station one night with his friends, poisoned a farmer's milk herd, set fifty acres of woods on fire. One night, racing, he turned too wide and drove his Chevy Malibu into the living room of a house. But he wasn't hurt. Nothing ever happened to him. He had a juvenile record and was headed, my mother said, for the other side of the green grass, when, the day he turned eighteen, like a boiling pot coming off the fire, he just stopped.

It didn't seem that anybody just changed like that, but evidently Lawrence did. This was how my mother told it. "The candle of the wicked shall be put out," she said. I was seven years old then. Lawrence was supposed to move from the house but she let him stay, and some sense just clicked on in his head. He stopped going out and his friends started calling him less, then stopped calling him completely. He cut his hair and bought a set of barbells that he lifted every evening, standing shirtless in the window of his room.

A few years later, when I was in junior high and after he had bought his computer, he began telling me to stay out of trouble. I had never gotten into any, though. I didn't want to steal cars or hit people. "It's not something I want to do," I told him.

"You will, though," he said. He looked at me. "That's for sure—you *will*. But be careful when you do." Then, to show me that he had said something serious, he put his left hand behind him. My mother had taken tranquilizers when she was pregnant with Lawrence, and now his hand had only two fingers. He always held it behind his back when he said something important. The lame fingers were wide at the knuckles and tapered at the ends, and the skin over them was shiny and waxlike. I hardly noticed it anymore. I remember my mother had once told me that Lawrence's hand was my father's legacy. She said this was how my father lived on in our lives.

I didn't understand at the time. "What do you mean?" I asked.

"It's cloven," she said.

On our family trip every June we drove for two weeks. The summer Lawrence left we started west through Nebraska and Wyoming, then south, through Utah and the Arizona desert, where we drove with wet towels hanging in the open windows. We headed west, over the Colorado River where it was wide, then back again, into canyonland, where the earth turned red and the mesas were veined with color. Darienne held a sketch pad on her knees and drew the cypress that clung to ledges in the escarpments. We turned north, into Utah, where mirages rose off the salt beds and in the distance the mountains were topped with snow. Whenever we stopped, my mother and Mrs. Silver and Darienne went on collecting trips. They came back with pieces of wood, dried seed pods, rocks with flecks of silver in them or with edges that looked polished. Darienne showed them to Lawrence. He stood at the side of the road, smoking, one hand on the open door of the car, while she went through what they had found. A rock that looked like a face, a flower that had dried to powdery maroon. He puffed on his cigarette, looked at the things she showed him. Then he got back into the car.

"The problem with our sister," he told me one day as we were drinking root beer at a gas station outside Salt Lake City, "is that she doesn't know what to do with what she knows." Darienne and Mrs. Silver and my mother were across the road sitting on a fence. Lawrence leaned over and picked a leaf from a patch of iceplant that was growing along the station lot. "Take this iceplant," he said. "Now, what would Dary say about it? That it's the color of the sea or something." He looked at me. "But what would you say about it?"

"That it's a succulent and stores water."

"That's right."

That night we drove until dawn. Darienne and my mother and Mrs. Silver slept in the back while I sat in front with Lawrence. The Great Salt Lake lay somewhere to the side of us, and I watched for it in the moonlight but could not tell it from the salt flats that extended everywhere around, gray and white and as unbroken as lake water. The mountains were gone by early morning. Then mesas appeared, and canyonland, and the road began to climb and dip. Behind us the sky was whitening. Lawrence quizzed me on the motorcycle engine. Then we were silent, the wheels clicking over the expansion fissures in the road.

He turned to me. "Knowledge is power," he said.

"I know."

"I'm going to go out and get that power." He tapped the wheel a couple of times. "I'm going out to California."

He hadn't ever mentioned leaving before. I looked over at him. "That's it," I said. "That's what you were going to tell me."

"Nope."

In fact, he had left Point Bluff once, a few years earlier. But it was only for the summer, when he went to work in Chicago. That was the only time he had ever been gone. He came home once or twice a month. One weekend when he didn't come home he had invited Darienne and me to come see him. He wrote that he would take Darienne to one of the world's great art museums and me to the Cubs game, but my mother wouldn't let us go. She said she didn't trust Chicago. "The Bible has spoken of such cities," she said. "If he wants to see you, he can come back here." He stayed away three months.

"When are you going to be back?"

"I'm going to stay out there a while," he said. "I'm getting into computers. I haven't told anybody yet, Edgar."

"Where will you go?"

"Silicon Valley," he said. "You ought to see it."

"You going to stay out there forever?"

"I'll be back."

"When?"

He sprayed the windshield three times with the automatic washer, then ran the wiper. "Edgar," he said. "You're not thinking about what's important."

I looked ahead of us. There were mobile homes scattered at the roadside. I never knew exactly what he meant when he said that. I tried to think what a twenty-seven-year-old would be thinking. "Are you meeting a girl?"

"Nope."

We drove on. Now the road was jet black in front of us, new asphalt. It was going underneath without noise. I thought about him leaving. Twenty-seven was old to be living in the basement, but I'd had the feeling now for a while that our family was different from other families. Other families we knew went to lakes in the summer. They threw wedding parties. It didn't seem that anybody in our family could ever get married. It didn't seem that anybody could leave.

"Computers are hot," I said.

"That's right."

"And you're good at them."

"I'm great at them."

"Lawrence," I said, "what's Mom going to do?"

He turned around and looked at the three of them asleep in the back. Then he looked straight ahead over the wheel again. He lowered his voice. "If I told you something, would you keep it quiet?"

I nodded.

He motioned his head toward the back seat. "I don't care what Mom does."

"What?"

He stared ahead.

"What?" I said again. I looked at him sitting next to me. He had the half-Indian nose Darienne gave my father in her paintings. Underneath it his stubble was unclipped. His skin was pocked from old acne. I tried to think, I tried to think *hard*, whether I cared about my mother. Then I looked up. "You sound like a bastard," I said.

He turned to me. "Bingo," he said. He clapped his hands

together under the wheel. "That's something important. I *am* a bastard."

I picked my fingernails.

"That's not what I was going to tell you, though." He pointed to his head. "But at least you're thinking. I'll tell you something else, though, right now."

"What is it?"

He held the wheel with his knees and put his arms behind his head. Then he glanced behind us. "I slept with Mrs. Silver," he said.

"What?"

He put his hands back on the wheel and whistled the opening of the Bellini oboe concerto. I looked behind us.

"You did not."

"I sure did. In the basement."

For some reason, although it had nothing to do with Mrs. Silver, I thought again about whether I really cared about my mother. Then I thought about whether I really cared about anybody. Then I thought about Mrs. Silver. I put my arm across the seatback. "Did you really?"

"Women are afraid of getting old," he said.

"So?"

"So, you play on that."

I tried to look behind us again without turning my neck. Mrs. Silver was asleep with her head leaning back over the seat. Her mouth was open and I saw her throat. She was married to a drunk. I knew that much. I also knew that her husband had been in prison. I paused while we passed some telephone poles. "That's what you were going to tell me, isn't it?"

"Nope."

I couldn't imagine what could be more important than that. Mrs. Silver's throat was white as bath soap, and she was in our house practically every day. When she waxed her legs they shone like my polished clutch plates. I looked at the road and tried to think of what it was like. I imagined waking up one night in my room to find her at the side of my bed, whispering. "Edgar," she would say. Her voice would be low and soft. "Edgar, I can't resist." At a party that year I had felt the breasts of a girl two grades ahead of me.

That afternoon Lawrence and I were in a gas station bathroom. We were drying our hands under the heat fan. "Lawrence," I said. I rubbed my hands together a few times. "Did *she* ask *you?*"

"Did who ask me?"

"You know," I said. The dryer stopped and I put my hands in my pockets. "Did Mrs. Silver ask *you?*"

"In a way."

"In what way?"

"In the way women ask for a thing."

"How do women ask for a thing?"

He walked out to the parking lot and I followed him. We were in the desert. The tar was soft under my shoes, and Darienne and my mother and Mrs. Silver sat on towels on the car hood. Mrs. Silver was wearing a halter top tied high over her abdomen. "They ask for a thing by making you think of it," said Lawrence.

When we got home from our trip that year I started my diary. I hadn't written anything in it before. It was leatherette, with my initials embossed, and it locked. The key was attached by a piece of yellow string. I opened it and reread the inscription. Then I turned to the first page.

JUNE 21st—

I wrote.

LAWRENCE IS LEAVING.

I thought of writing about Mrs. Silver. I closed the diary and locked it, then got a paper clip from the desk. When I tried it, the paper clip opened the lock. I decided not to write about her.

Darienne knocked on the door and came in. "I have to tell you something," she said. She looked at my desk. "You're using that," she said.

"What did you have to tell me?"

"That you can't tell anybody about the cyanide." She stepped behind me. "And you can't write about it, either."

"Why not?"

"It's not even cyanide," she said. "It's a diet pill. You wrote about it, didn't you?"

"Maybe."

"Let me see."

I closed the diary and locked it. She took two oboe reeds from her shirt pocket and put them in her mouth. "You ought to wash those first," I said.

"I knew you'd already written about it."

"I have not. And what do you care if I did?"

"I don't want Lawrence to know. I want him to remember good things about me."

"What if he does know? He knows everything else about you."

"He does not."

"It doesn't matter," I said.

"It does so."

I looked at her. There was always something about her that made me angry. I didn't know what it was. She looked at me as if I were about to hit her. I turned and faced right into her eyes. "It doesn't matter," I said, "because he hates you anyway."

She stepped back and felt for the door handle, and for a moment I thought she was actually going to fall. Then she left, and I didn't see her again until that afternoon, when she came outside to the yard. Lawrence and I were patching the muffler. She stood off to the side of us, humming the Bellini concerto. Even when she hummed, she repeated parts, went over and over bars as if she were practicing. It was a warm afternoon and I didn't want anything to bother me. I was cutting squares of fiber-glass mesh to fit the rust holes in the tailpipe. Lawrence was mixing the hardener. Darienne stopped and repeated a phrase. Then she repeated it again, louder.

"Hi, Dary," I said.

"Hi, Edgar. Hi, Lawrence."

"You're crossing railroad tracks," Lawrence said.

"What?" said Darienne.

"You're crossing a set of railroad tracks," he said, "when the car you're driving stalls." He squeezed out a ribbon of fiber-glass putty onto the plastic spatula and mixed it with hardener. Darienne had stopped humming. "You look up and see that around the bend the locomotive is coming. You're right in the middle of the track and the engineer won't see you in time to stop." He picked up the mixture with a spreader and pressed it into the dent in the rear of the tailpipe. "What are you going to do?"

"Start the car," said Darienne.

"It won't start."

"Give it gas."

"It still won't start. The train is coming," he said. He looked at me.

I cut four neat corners on a square of mesh. "Get out of the car," I answered.

"Bingo," said Lawrence.

Darienne took a step toward us, reached with her leg, and kicked our parts tray upside down. "You'll never get a job with that hand," she said.

Lawrence laughed. "What did you say?"

"It's a beautiful day out here," I said.

"I said you'll never get a job with that hand of yours."

Lawrence turned around in his crouch. "Damn you," he whispered. He gathered up a couple of bolts that had rolled next to him. Then he picked up a hammer from the tool chest. So quickly that it seemed to be done by someone else, not by any of us, but by a fourth, by another person, he grabbed Darienne and threw her to the ground. She hit hard on her hip. She was alongside the motorcycle, on her side in the dirt, and he raised the hammer over her face. For a moment its shiny head was above us. My brother's arm was cocked back, stiff with anger. I watched it. I saw the hair and the sweat on his wrist. I saw the hammer's rubber handle and the red steel of its shaft. AMERICAN BEAUTY HARDWARE, it said. The words were printed on aluminum tape wrapped at the neck. There was a rose emblem, black and silver, at the top. At the height of his swing it reflected brilliant light. I didn't say anything. I stood behind them. Darienne screamed. I stepped forward and grabbed Lawrence's hand.

His arm relaxed, and while Darienne scrambled up beside him he let the hammer fall from his grip. Darienne stood. Her skirt was marked with dust and oil. She brushed her cheeks, first one, then the other. Then she turned around and ran into the house.

I turned the parts tray over and began picking up springs and bolts. "Jesus, Lawrence," I said.

"She'll get over it."

In front of me, in the pan, bits of dust floated on the oil. "But you wouldn't have hit her."

"Probably not."

"You can't hit somebody like that." I looked up at him and smiled. "Come on."

He picked up the hammer and put it back in the toolbox. "What the hell would *you* know about anything?" he said.

We brought Lawrence to the bus station the week before baseball camp started. He left Darienne's painting behind because, he said, he would be back to get it. After breakfast we hung it in the living room. Lawrence said goodbye to Caramel and we got into my mother's Dodge and drove to the station.

When the bus came I helped him on with his stuff. The driver put his duffel underneath and I carried his small suitcase, which had been our father's, into the coach for him. The bus was blue inside and smelled of smoke. It didn't have a skylight. Lawrence took a seat toward the back, next to a middle-aged woman. The driver got back in. I could see Darienne and my mother waiting at the front door. Lawrence went up the aisle and kissed my mother. I watched Darienne let him kiss her also. I got out.

When the bus started to move my mother held Darienne's arm. "When will he be back?" asked Darienne.

"He walked in all the ways of his father," said my mother.

"Dary, you're not thinking about what's important," I said.

We watched the bus go out to the highway before we got back in our car. On the ride home we stopped for ice cream cones. That evening Mrs. Silver came over and drank vodka cranberries with my mother in the back yard. I drank one too, without ice, and it made me a little drunk. Darienne stayed inside.

I sat on an aluminum chair, my hands tingling from the liquor, and thought of a time when I would barely remember my brother. He would be in California in two days. Then, for as long as I could imagine, I would be living in this house with my mother and my sister. I knew I would never finish the motorcycle. It would lie out in the yard and the rust would eventually enter the engine. But that didn't bother me. I looked at my mother. She was stirring the ice in her glass. Darienne was probably upstairs drawing one line and then another, changing the shading, changing the edge. The light was fading. It seemed to me that all of them, she and my mother and Lawrence, had suffered a wound that had somehow skipped over me. I drank more of my vodka cranberry. Life seemed okay to me. It seemed okay even now, the day my brother left. It even seemed pleasant, which was the way, despite everything she said, I thought it probably seemed to Mrs. Silver.

I looked at her. She was leaning back on a lounger, reading the newspaper. She didn't seem upset about Lawrence leaving. But that's what I would have expected. She wasn't like my mother, and she wasn't like Darienne or Lawrence. Life just flowed over her. It melted over her like wax. I wondered if *she* cared about anybody. She looked up at me then, as I sat watching her, and I saw that her mouth was rimmed with cranberry.

I smiled. She smiled back. I stood up and went into the house, and after I looked at our new painting for a while I walked upstairs to see my sister. When I came into her room the lights were off except for the Bambi nightlight. It lit the baseboard. In its small, yellow glow I could see Darienne on the bed. Her white legs were drawn up against her chest and she was crying. I went over and sat next to her.

"Hi, Dary."

She didn't say anything. We sat there for a while. She rocked up and back against the wall.

"You shouldn't be so sad," I said. "He was a pecker to you."

"I don't care."

We sat for a few minutes. I thought about things. Then I leaned back next to her. "Dary," I said, "you are driving on a very hot day." I could smell the herbal shampoo in her hair.

"A day in which it is over one hundred degrees outside, when you notice halfway up a mountain grade that the temperature gauge on the dashboard indicates hot." I got up from the bed, took a couple of steps across the room, came back. I picked the dirt from my fingernails. "What are you going to do?"

"Edgar, I'm your older sister."

"Come on."

She pulled her knees up.

"The car is overheating."

"I don't know what to do," she said.

I sat lower on the bed again. The two of us pushed together on the quilt. Then, next to her, I started to cry too. I was thinking of Lawrence. Last night I had gone down to his apartment to see him. I almost never went in there. The computer was in a box and his clothes were folded in stacks on the bed. The door was open and the sun was setting, so we went and stood together on the steps. He picked up pebbles from his entranceway and threw them into the yard.

"Have a good time," I said.

"I will."

"When will you visit?"

"I may not be back for a while," he said.

"Not for a while."

"That's right."

"I'll finish the Honda."

"Good."

Then Darienne came down from the house. She walked past Lawrence and stood between us. "I have something to ask you, Edgar," she said.

"What is it?"

"I want to know whether he was going to hit me."

I laughed. I looked at Lawrence's back.

"Tell me," she said.

I laughed again. "Were you going to hit her?" I said to Lawrence.

"I asked *you*," said Darienne.

"You can't ask me that, Dary," I said. "You can't just ask me whether another person was going to do something." I put my hand on her arm.

"Tell me," she said.

"Dary, I can't tell you that. I can tell you what *I* would have done." I leaned down and picked up a couple of pebbles. "But Dary, you knocked over our parts. They're covered with dirt now. There's gravel in the transmission. I can't tell you what Lawrence would or wouldn't do."

"Would he have hit me?"

"I can't tell you that."

Lawrence tossed a pebble over the hedge. "Tell her what you think," he said.

She looked into my eyes. I wanted to change the subject, but I couldn't think of anything to say. I smiled. I really tried to think about it. "Yes," I said. "I think he would have."

Darienne turned and went back into the house. I stayed behind Lawrence. Even from the back I thought he was smiling. I threw the pebbles in my palm one by one over the hedge.

"Do you think *you* would have hit her?" he said. He didn't turn around.

"No," I answered.

He chuckled. I thought he was going to say something more, but he didn't. He let the pebbles drop from his hand.

"You know what I'm waiting for?" I asked.

"You're waiting for me to tell you what I was going to tell you."

"That's right."

"Well," he said. "This is it." He turned around and faced me. "You're a bastard, too," he said.

"What?"

"I mean, yes, you would have hit her too. You just don't know it yet." He pointed at me. "But if something ever goes wrong, you're going to turn into a son of a bitch, just like me." He smiled slightly. "Just like every guy in the world. You don't know it yet because everything's all right so far. You think you're a nice guy and that everything hasn't really affected you. But you can't get away from it." He tapped his chest. "It's in your blood."

"That's what you were going to tell me?"

"Bingo," he said.

Then he brushed past me and went into his apartment. I followed and stood behind him in the doorway. A wind had come up and I put my hands into my pockets. He stood with his back to me, placing shirts into a box, not saying anything. He was wearing a jean jacket and chino pants with pleats. We were silent, standing in his darkening apartment, and I tried to imagine what the world was like for him.

THE CARNIVAL DOG,
THE BUYER
OF DIAMONDS

◆ ◆ ◆

W HAT'S THE ONE THING you should never do? Quit?
Depends on who you talk to. Steal? Cheat? Eat food
from a dented can? Myron Lufkin's father, Abe, once told
him never get your temperature taken at the hospital. Bring
your own thermometer, he said; you should see how they
wash theirs. He ought to have known; when he was at Ye-
shiva University he worked as an orderly in the hospital, slid
patients around on gurneys, cleaned steelware. Myron knows
all his father's hospital stories and all his rules. On the other
hand, there are things you *should* do. Always eat sitting
down. Wear a hat in the rain. What else? Never let the other
guy start the fight. Certain inviolable commandments. In
thirty-two years Myron Lufkin had never seen his father
without an answer.

That is, until the day five years ago when Myron called
home from Albert Einstein College of Medicine and told his
father he had had enough, was quitting, leaving, *kaput,* he
said. Now, Myron, living in Boston, sometime Jew, member
of the public gym where he plays basketball and swims in
the steamy pool after rounds, still calls home every other
week. The phone calls, if he catches his father asleep, remind
him of the day five years ago when he called to say that he
was not, after all, going to be a doctor.

It was not the kind of thing you told Abe Lufkin. Abe
Lufkin, a man who once on Election Day put three twelve-
pound chains across his chest and dove into San Francisco Bay
at Aquatic Park, to swim most of the mile and three-quarters
across to Marin. As it turned out they had to pull him from
the frothy cold water before he made the beach—but to give
him credit, he was not a young man. In the *Chronicle* the next
day there he was on an inside page, sputtering and shaking
on the sand, steam rising off his body. Rachel, Myron's
mother, is next to him in a sweater and baggy wool pants.
Myron still has the newspaper clipping in one of his old but-
terfly display cases wrapped in tissue paper in a drawer in
Boston.

On the day Myron called home from Albert Einstein to say
that three years of studying and money, three years of his
life, had been a waste, he could imagine the blood-rush in
his father's head. But he knew what to expect. He kept firm,
though he could feel the pulse in his own neck. Itzhak, his
roommate at medical school, had stood behind him with his
hand on Myron's shoulder, smoking a cigarette. But Abe
simply did not believe it.

Myron didn't expect him to believe it: Abe, after all, didn't
understand quitting. If his father had been a sea captain,
Myron thought, he would have gone down with his ship—
singing, boasting, denying the ocean that closed over his
head—and this was not, in Myron's view, a glorious death.
It just showed stubbornness. His father was stubborn about
everything. When he was young, for example, when stickball
was what you did in the Bronx, Abe played basketball. Almost nobody else played. In those days, Abe told Myron, you
went to the Yankee games when Detroit was in town and
rooted for Hank Greenberg to hit one out, and when he did
you talked about it and said how the *goyishe* umpires would
have ruled it foul if they could have, if it hadn't been to
center field. In Abe's day, baseball was played by men named

McCarthy, Murphy, and Burdock, and basketball wasn't really played at all, except by the very very tall, awkward kids. But not Abe Lufkin. He was built like a road-show wrestler and he kept a basketball under his bed. It was his love for the game, maybe, that many years later made him decide to have a kid. When Myron was born, Abe nailed a backboard to the garage. This is my boy, he said, my *mensch*. He began playing basketball with his son when Myron was nine. But really, what they did was not playing. By the time Myron was in the fifth grade Abe had visions in his already balding pharmacist's head. He sat in the aluminum lawn furniture before dinner and counted out the one hundred layups Myron had to do from each side of the basket. One hundred from the left. One hundred from the right. No misses.

But it paid off. At Woodrow Wilson High, Myron was the star. Myron hitting a twenty-foot bank shot. Myron slipping a blind pass inside, stealing opponents' dribbles so their hands continued down, never realizing the ball was gone. Myron blocking the last-second shot. It was a show. Before the games he stood alone under the basket, holding his toes and stretching loose the muscles in his thighs. He knew Abe was sitting in the stands. His father always got there before the teams even came upstairs to the gym. He took the front-row seat at one corner and made Rachel take the one at the opposite corner. Then at halftime they switched. This way Abe could always see the basket his son was shooting at. After the games Abe waited in the car for Myron. Rachel sat in the back, and when Myron got in, Abe talked about the game until the windows steamed or Rachel finally said that it was unhealthy to sit like this in the cold. Then Abe wiped the windows and started the car, and they drove home with the heater blasting up warm air between the seats.

Abe had always believed the essence of the body was in the lungs, and sometimes, to keep Myron in shape for basketball, he challenged him to breath-holding contests. They sat facing each other across the kitchen table without breathing while an egg timer ran down between them. Myron could never beat his father, though; Abe held his breath like a blowfish at low tide. Myron's eyes teared, his heart pounded in his head, his lungs swelled to combustion, while all the time his father just stared at him, winking. He made Myron admit defeat out loud. "Do you give?" Abe whispered when half the sand had run down through the timer. Myron swallowed, pressed his lips together, stared at the sand falling through the narrow neck. A few seconds later, Abe said it again: "Do you give?" Myron squeezed his legs together, held his hands over his mouth, stood up, sat down, and finally let his breath explode out. "I give," he said, then sat there until the egg timer ran down and Abe exhaled.

There was always this obsession in the Lufkin family, this holiness about the affairs of the body. What were wars or political speeches next to the importance of body heat, expansive lungs, or leg muscles that could take you up the stairs instead of the elevator? Abe told hospital stories because to him there was no more basic truth than keeping your bronchial tubes cleared, or drying between your toes. Any questions of the body were settled quickly and finally when Abe showed Myron the smelly fungus between his own toes, or opened the *Encyclopaedia Britannica* to pictures of stomach worms, syphilis, or skin rash.

Any religious fervor in the family went instead into this worship of the body. Rachel did not light candles on Friday nights, and Myron was never *bar-mitzvahed*. Instead there was health to be zealous about. It was Abe's way. But at times he wavered, and these were nearly the only times Myron ever saw him unsure—in the evenings when he read the newspaper and talked about the State of Israel, or on Friday nights sometimes when he stood in the living room with the lights off, staring out at the sidewalk as the congregation filtered by in wool coats and *yarmulkes*. It put Abe into a mood. The spring after Myron's fifteenth birthday he told Myron he was sending him to a Judaism camp in the mountains for the month of July. They were outside on the porch when Abe told him.

"What? A Judaism camp? I don't believe it."

"What don't you believe?"

"I'm not going to a Judaism camp."

"What's this? Yes, you're going. You've got no more religion than *goyim*. I've already sent the money."

"How much money?"

"Fifty dollars."

Then Abe went in from the porch, and that was the end of the argument. Myron knew he would have to go off in the hot, bright month of July. That was how Abe argued. He wasn't wordy. If you wanted to change his mind you didn't argue, you fought him with your fists or your knees. This was what he expected from the world, and this was what he taught his son. Once, when Myron was fourteen, Abe had taken him to a bar, and when the bouncer hadn't wanted to let him in Abe said, "This is my *mensch;* he's not going to drink," and had pushed Myron in front of him through the door. Later, when they stood in line to pee away their drinks, Abe told him you can do what you want with strangers because they don't want to fight. "Remember that," he said.

But the day after he told Myron about the Judaism camp, Abe came out on the porch and said, "Myron, you're a man now and we're going to decide about camp like men."

"What?"

"We're going to decide like men. We're going to have a race."

"We can't race."

"What do you mean, we can't race? We sure can. A footrace, from here to the end of the block. I win, you go to camp."

"I don't want to do it."

"What, do you want it longer? We can do what you want. We can make it two times to the corner."

Then Abe went into the house, and Myron sat on the porch. He didn't want to learn religion during the hottest month of the year, but also, he knew, there was something in beating his father that was like the toppling of an ancient king. What was it for him to race an old man? He walked down to the street, stretched the muscles in his legs, and sprinted up to the corner. He sprinted back down to the house, sat down on the steps, and decided it wasn't so bad to go to the mountains in July. That afternoon Abe came out of the house in long pants and black, rubber-soled shoes, and he and Myron lined up on one of the sidewalk lines and raced, and Abe won going away. The sound of Abe's fierce breathing and his hard shoes pounding the cement hid the calmness of Myron's own breath. That July Myron packed Abe's old black cloth traveling bag and got on the bus to the mountains.

But what Abe taught Myron was more than just competition; it was everything. It was the way he got to work every day for thirty-seven years without being late, the way he treated Rachel, his bride of uncountable years, who sewed, cooked, cleaned for him, in return for what? For Sunday night dinners out every single week, a ritual so ancient that Myron couldn't break it even after he moved out of the house. For Sunday dinners out, and a new diamond each year. It was a point of honor, an expectation. Obviously on a pharmacist's salary Abe couldn't afford it. He bought her rings, necklaces, bracelets, brooches, hairpins, earrings, lockets—one gift at the end of each year for, what is it, almost forty years? One year Rachel was sick with mild hepatitis and spent the holidays in the hospital. On the first evening of Chanukah Abe took Myron with him to visit her, and in the hospital room he pulled out a small bracelet strung with a diamond and gave it to her, his wife, as she lay in the bed. But what is the value of a diamond, he later asked Myron in the car, next to the health of the body?

It was two years later that Abe tried the swim across San Francisco Bay. But there were other things before that. At the age of fifty-four he fought in a bar over politics. Yes, fought. He came home with his knuckles wrapped in a handkerchief. On his cheek there was a purple bruise that even over the years never disappeared, only gradually settled down the side of his face and formed a black blotch underneath his jaw. That was when he told Myron never to let the other guy start the fight. Always get the first punch, he said. Myron was sixteen then, sitting in the kitchen watching his father rub iodine into the split skin behind his knuckles. The smell stayed in the kitchen for days, the smell of hospitals that later came to be the smell of all his father's clothes, and of his closet. Maybe Myron had just never noticed it before, but on that day his father began to smell old.

Myron was startled. Even then he had been concerned with life. He was a preserver, a collector of butterflies that he caught on the driving trips the family took in the summers. The shelves in his bedroom were lined with swallowtails and monarchs pressed against glass panes, the crystal dust still on their wings. Later, in college, he had studied biology, zoology, entomology, looking inside things, looking at life. Once, on a driving trip through Colorado when Myron was young, Abe had stopped the car near the lip of a deep gorge. Across from where they got out and stood, the cliffs extended down a quarter of a mile, colored with clinging green brush, wildflowers, shafts of red clay, and, at the bottom, a turquoise river. But there were no animals on the sheer faces, no movement anywhere in the gorge. Abe said that life could survive anywhere, even on cliffs like these, and that this was a miracle. But Myron said nothing. To him, anything that couldn't move, that couldn't fly or swim or run, was not really alive. Real life interested him. His father interested him, with his smells and exertions, with the shifting bruise on his jaw.

Years later, on his first day at Albert Einstein medical school, the thing Myron noticed was the smell, the pungency of the antiseptics, like the iodine Abe had once rubbed into his knuckles. On that first day when a whole class of new medical students listened to an address by the dean of the medical college, the only thing Myron noticed was that the room smelled like his father.

Medical school was a mountain of facts, a giant granite peak full of outcroppings and hidden crevices. Physiology. Anatomy. Histology. More facts than he could ever hope to remember. To know the twenty-eight bones of the hand seemed to Myron a rare and privileged knowledge, but then there were the arms and shoulders with their bones and tendons and opposing muscles, then the whole intricate, extravagant cavity of the chest, and then the head and the abdomen and the legs. Myron never really tried to learn it all. It wasn't the volume of knowledge so much as it was the place where he had to be in order to learn it. The anatomy labs reeked of formaldehyde, the hospitals of a mixture of cleanliness and death. All of it reminded Myron of men getting old, and that is why in three years of medical school he made the minuscule but conscious effort not to study enough. He let the knowledge collect around him, in notebooks, binders, pads, on napkins and checks, everywhere except in his brain. His room was strewn with notes he never studied. Once in a letter home he said learning medicine was like trying to drink water from a fire hose.

But that was something Abe would want to hear. Once on a driving trip through the Florida deltas, Abe came upon three men trying to lift an abandoned car from a sludge pit with a rope they had looped around it. Only the roof and the tops of the windows were showing above the mud, but Abe got out anyway and helped the men pull. His face turned red and the muscles in his belly shook so much Myron could see them through his shirt. Myron didn't understand the futility of his father's effort, or even know why he helped save a useless car for men he didn't know, until years later. Abe did things like that; he loved doing things like that.

Myron, on the other hand, just didn't want to study. His weren't the usual reasons for quitting medical school. It wasn't the hours, and really, it wasn't the studying and the studying. It was something smaller, harder, that in a vague way he knew had to do with Abe. Perhaps he saw his own father in the coughing middle-aged men whose hearts he watched flutter across oscilloscope screens. But it was not Abe's death that he feared. Heart stoppage or brain tumors or sudden clots of blood were reactions of the body, and thus, he had always believed, they were good. Death, when it was a fast action, didn't bother him. The fatty cadavers in anatomy labs were no more than objects to Myron, and it meant nothing to him that they were dead. The only time in his life that he had had to really think about death was in his childhood, when the phone rang in the middle of the night to tell Abe about his aunt in Miami Beach. The next morning Myron had found his father downstairs drinking coffee. "Life is for the living," Abe had said, and even then Myron could weigh the seriousness in his voice. It was plain that death meant only a little if you still had the good muscles in your own heart, and that people's bodies, once under ground, were not to be mourned. And besides, there really was no blood in the medical school anatomy classes. The cadavers were gray, no different when you cut them than the cooked leg of a turkey. They had none of the pliable fleshiness, none of the pink, none of the smells and secretions that told you of life.

No, it wasn't death that bothered Myron; it was the downhill plunge of the living body—the muscles that stretched off the bones into folds, the powdery flesh odors of middle-aged men. He longed for some octogenarian to stand up suddenly from a wheelchair and run the length of a corridor. Once, a drugged coronary patient, a sixty-year-old man, had unhooked an IV cart and caromed on it through the corridor until Myron cornered him. When Myron looked at the blood spots that were in the old man's eyes, he wanted to take him in his own arms then and there, in his triumph. That was why Myron wanted to quit medical school. He hated the demise of the spirit.

So he let the work pile up around him. In his third year he felt the walls of the lecture halls and the sponged hospital floors to be somehow holding him against his will. Fifty-year-old men who could no longer walk, or whose intestines bled and collapsed, Myron felt, were betrayers of the human race. He was convinced of the mind's control over the flesh.

In the winter of his third year he started jogging. First two, three miles a day, then, later, long six-mile runs into the hills and neighborhoods around the medical school. He left in the early mornings and ran in the frozen air so that he could feel the chill in his lungs. He ran every morning through November and December, and then January after the holidays, until one morning in February, when the grass was still breaking like needles underneath his feet, he realized he could run forever. That morning he just kept running. He imagined Itzhak sitting with two cups of coffee at the table, but he ran to the top of a hill and watched the streets below him fill with morning traffic. Then onward he went, amidst the distant bleating of car horns and the whistling wind. He thought of the hospital, of the arriving interns, sleepless, pale, and of the third-year students following doctors from room to room. He ran on the balls of his feet and never got tired.

When he returned to the apartment Itzhak was at the table eating lunch. Myron took a carton of milk from the refrigerator and drank standing up, without a glass.

"You ever think about passing infection that way?"

Myron put down the carton and looked at the muscles twitching in his thighs. Itzhak lit a cigarette.

"You're a real one," Itzhak said. "Where the hell were you?"

"Hypoxia. No oxygen to the brain. You know how easy it is to forget what time it is."

"Watch it," Itzhak said. "You'll get into trouble."

The next day Myron went to classes and to rounds, but that night he ran again, stumbling in the unlit paths, and after that, over the next weeks of frozen, windless days, he ran through his morning assignments and spent the afternoons in a park near his apartment. There was a basketball hoop there, a metal backboard with a chain net, and sometimes he shot with a group of kids or joined their half-court games. Afterward, he always ran again. He loved to sweat when the air was cold enough to turn the grass brittle, when a breath of air felt like a gulp of cold water. After a while, Itzhak began to ignore his disappearances. One day when Myron returned from running, Itzhak took his pulse. "Damn, Myron," he said, "you *are* running." His professors tried to take him aside, and Myron could see them looking into his pupils when they spoke. But he ignored them. One night he returned late from running, still dripping sweat, picked up the telephone and dialed, and heard his father's sleepy voice on the other end of the line. "Pa," he said, "it's *kaput* here."

So why the quitting now? Why the phone call at ten-thirty on a Thursday night when Abe and Rachel were just going into their dream sleep? Myron could hear the surprise, the speechlessness. He heard Rachel over the line telling Abe to calm himself, to give her the phone. He imagined the blood rushing to Abe's face, the breathing starting again the way he breathed the morning they pulled him from the frothy water in San Francisco Bay. Rachel took the phone and spoke, and Myron, because he had lived with his father for most of his life, knew Abe was taking black socks from the drawer and stretching them over his feet.

The next morning at seven Myron opened the apartment door and Abe was sitting there in a chair with the black cloth traveling bag on his lap. He was wide awake, blocking the passage out of the apartment.

"For crying out loud!"

"Who else did you expect? Am I supposed to let you throw away everything?"

"Pa, I didn't expect *anybody*."

"Well, I came, and I'm here, and I spent like a madman to get a flight. You think I don't have the lungs to argue with my son?"

"I was about to go running."

"I'll come along. We're going to settle this thing."

"Okay," Myron said, "come," and in his sweatsuit, hooded and wrapped against the cold, he led Abe down through the corridors of the building and out into the street. The ground outside was frozen from the night, the morning icy cold and without wind. Abe held the black traveling bag at his side as they stood under the entrance awning.

"I was planning to run." '

"It won't hurt you to walk a few blocks."

It was cold, so they walked quickly. Abe was wearing what he always wore in the winter, a black hat, gloves, galoshes, an overcoat that smelled of rain. Myron watched him out of the side of his vision. He tried to look at his father without turning around—at the face, at the black bruise under the jaw, at the shoulders. He tried to see the body beneath the clothing. Abe's arm swung with the weight of the traveling bag, and for the first time, as he watched through the corner of his eye, Myron noticed the faint spherical outline inside the cloth.

They walked wordlessly, Myron watching Abe's breath come out in clouds. By now the streets had begun to move with traffic, and the ice patches, black and treacherous, crackled underneath their feet. The streetlamps had gone off and in the distance dogs barked. They came to the park where Myron played basketball in the afternoons.

"So you brought the ball," Myron said.

"Maybe you want some shooting to calm you."

"You're not thinking of any games, are you?"

"I just brought it in case you wanted to shoot."

Abe unzipped the bag and pulled out the basketball. They went into the court. He bounced the ball on the icy pavement, then handed it to Myron. Myron spun it on his finger, dribbled it off the ice. He was watching Abe. He couldn't see beneath the overcoat, but Abe's face seemed drawn down, the cheeks puffier, the dark bruise lax on his jaw.

"Pa, why don't you shoot some? It would make you warm."

"You think you have to keep me warm? Look at this." He took off the overcoat. "Give me the ball."

Myron threw it to him, and Abe dribbled it in his gloved hands. Abe was standing near the free-throw line, and he turned then, brought the ball to his hip, and shot it, and as his back was turned to watch the shot, Myron did an incred-

ible thing—he crouched, took three lunging steps, and dove
into the back of his father's thin, tendoned knees. Abe
tumbled backward over him. What could have possessed Myron to do such a thing? A medical student, almost a doctor—
what the hell was he doing? But Myron knew his father. Abe
was a prizefighter, a carnival dog. Myron knew he would
protect the exposed part of his skull, that he would roll and
take the weight on his shoulders, that he would be up in-
stantly, crouched and ready to go at it. But Myron had slid
on the ice after the impact, and when he scrambled back up
and turned around, his father was on his back on the icy
pavement. He was flat out.

"Pa!"

Abe was as stiff and extended as Myron had ever seen a
human being. He was like a man who had laid out his own
body.

"What kind of crazy man are you?" Abe said hoarsely. "I
think it's broken."

"What? What's broken?"

"My back. You broke your old man's back."

"Oh no, Pa, I couldn't have! Can you move your toes?"

But the old man couldn't. He lay on the ground staring
up at Myron like a beached sea animal. Oh, Pa. Myron could
see the unnatural stiffness in his body, in the squat legs and
the hard, protruding belly.

"Look," Myron said, "don't move." Then he turned and
started back to get his father's coat, and he had taken one
step when Abe—Abe the carnival dog, the buyer of diamonds and the man of endurance—hooked his hand around
Myron's ankles and sent him tumbling onto the ice. Bastard!
Pretender! He scrambled up and pinned Myron's shoulders
against the pavement. "Faker!" Myron cried. He grappled
with the old man, butted him with his head and tried to
topple his balance, but Abe clung viciously and set the

weight of his chest against Myron's shoulders. "Fraud!" shouted Myron. "Cheat!" He shifted his weight and tried to roll Abe over, but his father's legs were spread wide and he had pinned Myron's hands. "Coward," Myron said. Abe's wrists pressed into Myron's arms. His knees dug into Myron's thighs. "Thief," Myron whispered. "Scoundrel." Cold water was spreading upward through Myron's clothes and Abe was panting hoarse clouds of steam into his face when Myron realized his father was leaning down and speaking into his ear.

"Do you give?"

"What?"

"Do you give?"

"You mean, will I go back to school?"

"That's what I mean."

"Look," Myron said, "you're crazy."

"Give me your answer."

Myron thought about this. While his father leaned down over him, pressed into him with his knees and elbows, breathed steam into his face, he thought about it. As he lay there he thought about other things too: This is my father, he thought. Then: This is my life. For a while, as the cold water spread through his clothes, he lay there and remembered things—the thousands and thousands of layups, the smell of a cadaver, the footrace on a bright afternoon in April. Then he thought: What can you do? These are clouds above us, and below us there is ice and the earth. He said, "I give."

STAR FOOD

◆ ◆ ◆

T HE SUMMER I turned eighteen I disappointed both my
parents for the first time. This hadn't happened before,
since what disappointed one usually pleased the other. As a
child, if I played broom hockey instead of going to school,
my mother wept and my father took me outside later to find
out how many goals I had scored. On the other hand, if I
spent Saturday afternoon on the roof of my parents' grocery
store staring up at the clouds instead of counting cracker
cartons in the stockroom, my father took me to the back to
talk about work and discipline, and my mother told me later
to keep looking for things that no one else saw.

This was her theory. My mother felt that men like Leo-
nardo da Vinci and Thomas Edison had simply stared long
enough at regular objects until they saw new things, and thus
my looking into the sky might someday make me a great
man. She believed I had a worldly curiosity. My father believed I wanted to avoid stock work.

Stock work was an issue in our family, as were all the jobs
that had to be done in a grocery store. Our store was called
Star Food and above it an incandescent star revolved. Its cir-
cuits buzzed, and its yellow points, as thick as my knees,
drooped with the slow melting of the bulb. On summer

nights flying insects flocked in clouds around it, droves of them burning on the glass. One of my jobs was to go out on the roof, the sloping, eaved side that looked over the western half of Arcade, California, and clean them off the star. At night, when their black bodies stood out against the glass, when the wind carried in the marsh smell of the New Jerusalem River, I went into the attic, crawled out the dormer window onto the peaked roof, and slid across the shingles to where the pole rose like a lightning rod into the night. I reached with a wet rag and rubbed away the June bugs and pickerel moths until the star was yellow-white and steaming from the moisture. Then I turned and looked over Arcade, across the bright avenue and my dimly lighted high school in the distance, into the low hills where oak trees grew in rows on the curbs and where girls drove to school in their own convertibles. When my father came up on the roof sometimes to talk about the store, we fixed our eyes on the red tile roofs or the small clouds of blue barbecue smoke that floated above the hills on warm evenings. While the clean bulb buzzed and flickered behind us, we talked about loss leaders or keeping the elephant-ear plums stacked in neat triangles.

The summer I disappointed my parents, though, my father talked to me about a lot of other things. He also made me look in the other direction whenever we were on the roof together, not west to the hills and their clouds of barbecue smoke, but east toward the other part of town. We crawled up one slope of the roof, then down the other so that I could see beyond the back alley where wash hung on lines in the moonlight, down to the neighborhoods across Route 5. These were the neighborhoods where men sat on the curbs on weekday afternoons, where rusted, wheel-less cars lay on blocks in the yards.

"*You're* going to end up on one of those curbs," my father told me.

Usually I stared farther into the clouds when he said something like that. He and my mother argued about what I did on the roof for so many hours at a time, and I hoped that by looking closely at the amazing borders of clouds I could confuse him. My mother believed I was on the verge of discovering something atmospheric, and I was sure she told my father this, so when he came upstairs, made me look across Route 5, and talked to me about how I was going to end up there, I squinted harder at the sky.

"You don't fool me for a second," he said.

He was up on the roof with me because I had been letting someone steal from the store.

From the time we first had the star on the roof, my mother believed her only son was destined for limited fame. Limited because she thought that true vision was distilled and could not be appreciated by everybody. I discovered this shortly after the star was installed, when I spent an hour looking out over the roofs and chimneys instead of helping my father stock a shipment of dairy. It was a hot day and the milk sat on the loading dock while he searched for me in the store and in our apartment next door. When he came up and found me, his neck was red and his footfalls shook the roof joists. At my age I was still allowed certain mistakes, but I'd seen the dairy truck arrive and knew I should have been downstairs, so it surprised me later, after I'd helped unload the milk, when my mother stopped beside me as I was sprinkling the leafy vegetables with a spray bottle.

"Dade, I don't want you to let anyone keep you from what you ought to be doing."

"I'm sorry," I said. "I should have helped with the milk earlier."

"No," she said, "that's not what I mean." Then she told me her theory of limited fame while I sprayed the cabbage and lettuce with the atomizer. It was the first time I had heard her idea. The world's most famous men, she said, presidents and emperors, generals and patriots, were men of vulgar fame, men who ruled the world because their ideas were obvious and could be understood by everybody. But there was also limited fame. Newton and Galileo and Enrico Fermi were men of limited fame, and as I stood there with the atomizer in my hand my mother's eyes watered over and she told me she knew in her heart that one day I was going to be a man of limited fame. I was twelve years old.

After that day I found I could avoid a certain amount of stock work by staying up on the roof and staring into the fine layers of stratus clouds that floated above Arcade. In the *Encyclopedia Americana* I read about cirrus and cumulus and thunderheads, about inversion layers and currents like the currents at sea, and in the afternoons I went upstairs and watched. The sky was a changing thing, I found out. It was more than a blue sheet. Twirling with pollen and sunlight, it began to transform itself.

Often as I stood on the roof my father came outside and swept the sidewalk across the street. Through the telephone poles and crossed power lines he looked up at me, his broom strokes small and fierce as if he were hoeing hard ground. It irked him that my mother encouraged me to stay on the roof. He was a short man with direct habits and an understanding of how to get along in the world, and he believed that God rewarded only two things, courtesy and hard work. God did not reward looking at the sky. In the car my father acknowledged good drivers and in restaurants he left good tips. He knew the names of his customers. He never sold a rotten vegetable. He shook hands often, looked everyone in the eye, and on Friday nights when we went to the movies he made us sit in the front row of the theater. "Why should I pay to look over other people's shoulders?" he said. The movies made him talk. On the way back to the car he walked with his hands clasped behind him and greeted everyone who passed. He smiled. He mentioned the fineness of the evening as if he were the admiral or aviator we had just seen on the screen. "People like it," he said. "It's good for business." My mother was quiet, walking with her slender arms folded in front of her as if she were cold.

I liked the movies because I imagined myself doing everything the heroes did—deciding to invade at daybreak, swimming half the night against the seaward current—but whenever we left the theater I was disappointed. From the front row, life seemed like a clear set of decisions, but on the street afterward I realized that the world existed all around me and I didn't know what I wanted. The quiet of evening and the ordinariness of human voices startled me.

Sometimes on the roof, as I stared into the layers of horizon, the sounds on the street faded into this same ordinariness. One afternoon when I was standing under the star my father came outside and looked up at me. "You're in a trance," he called. I glanced down at him, then squinted back at the horizon. For a minute he waited, and then from across the street he threw a rock. He had a pitcher's arm and could have hit me if he wanted, but the rock sailed past me and clattered on the shingles. My mother came right out of the store anyway and stopped him. "I wanted him off the roof," I heard my father tell her later in the same frank voice in which he explained his position to vegetable salesmen. "If someone's throwing rocks at him he'll come down. He's no fool."

I was flattered by this, but my mother won the point and from then on I could stay up on the roof when I wanted. To appease my father I cleaned the electric star, and though he often came outside to sweep, he stopped telling me to come down. I thought about limited fame and spent a lot of time noticing the sky. When I looked closely it was a sea with waves and shifting colors, wind seams and denials of distance, and after a while I learned to look at it so that it entered my eye whole. It was blue liquid. I spent hours looking into its pale wash, looking for things, though I didn't know what. I looked for lines or sectors, the diamond shapes of daylight stars. Sometimes, silver-winged jets from the air force base across the hills turned the right way against the sun and went off like small flash bulbs on the horizon. There was nothing that struck me and stayed, though, nothing with the brilliance of white light or electric explosion that I thought came with discovery, so after a while I changed my idea of discovery. I just stood on the roof and stared. When my mother asked me, I told her that I might be seeing new things but that seeing change took time. "It's slow," I told her. "It may take years."

The first time I let her steal I chalked it up to surprise. I was working the front register when she walked in, a thin, tall woman in a plaid dress that looked wilted. She went right to the standup display of cut-price, nearly expired breads and crackers, where she took a loaf of rye from the shelf. Then she turned and looked me in the eye. We were looking into each other's eyes when she walked out the front door. Through the blue-and-white LOOK UP TO STAR FOOD sign on the window I watched her cross the street.

There were two or three other shoppers in the store, and over the tops of the potato chip packages I could see my mother's broom. My father was in back unloading chicken parts. Nobody else had seen her come in; nobody had seen her leave. I locked the cash drawer and walked to the aisle where my mother was sweeping.

"I think someone just stole."

My mother wheeled a trash receptacle when she swept, and

as I stood there she closed it, put down her broom, and wiped her face with her handkerchief. "You couldn't get him?"

"It was a her."

"A lady?"

"I couldn't chase her. She came in and took a loaf of rye and left."

I had chased plenty of shoplifters before. They were kids usually, in sneakers and coats too warm for the weather. I chased them up the aisle and out the door, then to the corner and around it while ahead of me they tried to toss whatever it was—Twinkies, freeze-pops—into the sidewalk hedges. They cried when I caught them, begged me not to tell their parents. First time, my father said, scare them real good. Second time, call the law. I took them back with me to the store, held them by the collar as we walked. Then I sat them in the straight-back chair in the stockroom and gave them a speech my father had written. It was printed on a blue index card taped to the door. DO YOU KNOW WHAT YOU HAVE DONE? it began. DO YOU KNOW WHAT IT IS TO STEAL? I learned to pause between the questions, pace the room, check the card. "Give them time to get scared," my father said. He was expert at this. He never talked to them until he had dusted the vegetables or run a couple of women through the register. "Why should I stop my work for a kid who steals from me?" he said. When he finally came into the stockroom he moved and spoke the way policemen do at the scene of an accident. His manner was slow and deliberate. First he asked me what they had stolen. If I had recovered whatever it was, he took it and held it up to the light, turned it over in his fingers as if it were of large value. Then he opened the freezer door and led the kid inside to talk about law and punishment amid the frozen beef carcasses. He paced as he spoke, breathed clouds of vapor into the air.

In the end, though, my mother usually got him to let them off. Once when he wouldn't, when he had called the police to pick up a third-offense boy who sat trembling in the stockroom, my mother called him to the front of the store to talk to a customer. In the stockroom we kept a key to the back door hidden under a silver samovar that had belonged to my grandmother, and when my father was in front that afternoon my mother came to the rear, took it out, and opened the back door. She leaned down to the boy's ear. "Run," she said.

The next time she came in it happened the same way. My father was at the vegetable tier, stacking avocados. My mother was in back listening to the radio. It was afternoon. I rang in a customer, then looked up while I was putting the milk cartons in the bottom of the bag, and there she was. Her gray eyes were looking into mine. She had two cans of pineapple juice in her hands, and on the way out she held the door for an old woman.

That night I went up to clean the star. The air was clear. It was warm. When I finished wiping the glass I moved out over the edge of the eaves and looked into the distance where little turquoise squares—lighted swimming pools—stood out against the hills.

"Dade—"

It was my father's voice from behind the peak of the roof.

"Yes?"

"Come over to this side."

I mounted the shallow-pitched roof, went over the peak, and edged down the other slope to where I could see his silhouette against the lights on Route 5. He was smoking. I got up and we stood together at the edge of the shingled eaves. In front of us trucks rumbled by on the interstate, their trailers lit at the edges like the mast lights of ships.

"Look across the highway," he said.

"I am."

"What do you see?"

"Cars."

"What else?"

"Trucks."

For a while he didn't say anything. He dragged a few times on his cigarette, then pinched off the lit end and put the rest back in the pack. A couple of motorcycles went by, a car with one headlight, a bus.

"Do you know what it's like to live in a shack?" he said.

"No."

"You don't want to end up in a place like that. And it's damn easy to do if you don't know what you want. You know how easy it is?"

"Easy," I said.

"You have to know what you want."

For years my father had been trying to teach me competence and industry. Since I was nine I had been squeeze-drying mops before returning them to the closet, double-counting change, sweeping under the lip of the vegetable bins even if the dirt there was invisible to customers. On the basis of industry, my father said, Star Food had grown from a two-aisle, one-freezer corner store to the largest grocery in Arcade. When I was eight he had bought the failing gas station next door and built additions, so that now Star Food had nine aisles, separate coolers for dairy, soda, and beer, a tiered vegetable stand, a glass-fronted butcher counter, a part-time butcher, and, under what used to be the rain roof of the failing gas station, free parking while you shopped. When I started high school we moved into the apartment next door, and at meals we discussed store improvements.

Soon my father invented a grid system for easy location of foods. He stayed up one night and painted, and the next morning there was a new coordinate system on the ceiling of the store. It was a grid, A through J, 1 through 10. For weeks there were drops of blue paint in his eyelashes.

A few days later my mother pasted up fluorescent stars among the grid squares. She knew about the real constellations and was accurate with the ones she stuck to the ceiling, even though she also knew that the aisle lights in Star Food stayed on day and night, so that her stars were going to be invisible. We saw them only once, in fact, in a blackout a few months later, when they lit up in hazy clusters around the store.

"Do you know why I did it?" she asked me the night of the blackout as we stood beneath their pale light.

"No."

"Because of the idea."

She was full of ideas, and one was that I was accomplishing something on the shallow-pitched section of our roof. Sometimes she sat at the dormer window and watched me. Through the glass I could see the slender outlines of her cheekbones. "What do you see?" she asked. On warm nights she leaned over the sill and pointed out the constellations. "They are the illumination of great minds," she said.

After the woman walked out the second time I began to think a lot about what I wanted. I tried to discover what it was, and I had an idea it would come to me on the roof. In the evenings I sat up there and thought. I looked for signs. I threw pebbles down into the street and watched where they hit. I read the newspaper, and stories about ballplayers or jazz musicians began to catch my eye. When he was ten years old, Johnny Unitas strung a tire from a tree limb and spent afternoons throwing a football through it as it swung. Dizzy

Gillespie played with an orchestra when he was seven. There was an emperor who ruled China at age eight. What could be said about me? He swept the dirt no one could see under the lip of the vegetable bins.

The day after the woman had walked out the second time, my mother came up on the roof while I was cleaning the star. She usually wore medium heels and stayed away from the shingled roof, but that night she came up. I had been over the glass once when I saw her coming through the dormer window, skirt hem and white shoes lit by moonlight. Most of the insects were cleaned off and steam was drifting up into the night. She came through the window, took off her shoes, and edged down the roof until she was standing next to me at the star. "It's a beautiful night," she said.

"Cool."

"Dade, when you're up here do you ever think about what is in the mind of a great man when he makes a discovery?"

The night was just making its transition from the thin sky to the thick, the air was taking on weight, and at the horizon distances were shortening. I looked out over the plain and tried to think of an answer. That day I had been thinking about a story my father occasionally told. Just before he and my mother were married he took her to the top of the hills that surround Arcade. They stood with the New Jerusalem River, western California, and the sea on their left, and Arcade on their right. My father has always planned things well, and that day as they stood in the hill pass a thunderstorm covered everything west, while Arcade, shielded by hills, was lit by the sun. He asked her which way she wanted to go. She must have realized it was a test, because she thought for a moment and then looked to the right, and when they drove down from the hills that day my father mentioned the idea of a grocery. Star Food didn't open for a year after, but that was its conception, I think, in my father's mind. That afternoon as they stood with the New Jerusalem flowing below them, the plains before them, and my mother in a cotton skirt she had made herself, I think my father must have seen right through to the end of his life.

I had been trying to see right through to the end of my life, too, but these thoughts never led me in any direction. Sometimes I sat and remembered the unusual things that had happened to me. Once I had found the perfect, shed skin of a rattlesnake. My mother told my father that this indicated my potential for science. I was on the roof another time when it hailed apricot-size balls of ice on a summer afternoon. The day was hot and there was only one cloud, but as it approached from the distance it spread a shaft of darkness below it as if it had fallen through itself to the earth, and when it reached the New Jerusalem the river began throwing up spouts of water. Then it crossed onto land and I could see the hailstones denting parked cars. I went back inside the attic and watched it pass, and when I came outside again and picked up the ice balls that rolled between the corrugated roof spouts, their prickly edges melted in my fingers. In a minute they were gone. That was the rarest thing that had ever happened to me. Now I waited for rare things because it seemed to me that if you traced back the lives of men you arrived at some sort of sign, rainstorm at one horizon and sunlight at the other. On the roof I waited for mine. Sometimes I thought about the woman and sometimes I looked for silhouettes in the blue shapes between the clouds.

"Your father thinks you should be thinking about the store," said my mother.

"I know."

"You'll own the store some day."

There was a carpet of cirrus clouds in the distance, and we watched them as their bottom edges were gradually lit by the

rising moon. My mother tilted back her head and looked up
into the stars. "What beautiful names," she said. "Cassiopeia,
Lyra, Aquila."

"The Big Dipper," I said.

"Dade?"

"Yes?"

"I saw the lady come in yesterday."

"I didn't chase her."

"I know."

"What do you think of that?"

"I think you're doing more important things," she said.
"Dreams are more important than rye bread." She took the
bobby pins from her hair and held them in her palm. "Dade,
tell me the truth. What do you think about when you come
up here?"

In the distance there were car lights, trees, aluminum
power poles. There were several ways I could have answered.

I said, "I think I'm about to make a discovery."

After that my mother began meeting me at the bottom of
the stairs when I came down from the roof. She smiled ex-
pectantly. I snapped my fingers, tapped my feet. I blinked
and looked at my canvas shoe-tips. She kept smiling. I didn't
like this so I tried not coming down for entire afternoons,
but this only made her look more expectant. On the roof my
thoughts piled into one another. I couldn't even think of
something that was undiscovered. I stood and thought about
the woman.

Then my mother began leaving little snacks on the sill of
the dormer window. Crackers, cut apples, apricots. She arranged them in fan shapes or twirls on a plate, and after a
few days I started working regular hours again. I wore my
smock and checked customers through the register and went
upstairs only in the evenings. I came down after my mother

had gone to sleep. I was afraid the woman was coming back, but I couldn't face my mother twice a day at the bottom of the stairs. So I worked and looked up at the door whenever customers entered. I did stock work when I could, stayed in back where the air was refrigerated, but I sweated anyway. I unloaded melons, tuna fish, cereal. I counted the cases of freeze-pops, priced the cans of All-American ham. At the swinging door between the stockroom and the back of the store my heart went dizzy. The woman knew something about me.

In the evenings on the roof I tried to think what it was. I saw mysterious new clouds, odd combinations of cirrus and stratus. How did she root me into the linoleum floor with her gray stare? Above me on the roof the sky was simmering. It was blue gas. I knew she was coming back.

It was raining when she did. The door opened and I felt the wet breeze, and when I looked up she was standing with her back to me in front of the shelves of cheese and dairy, and this time I came out from the counter and stopped behind her. She smelled of the rain outside.

"Look," I whispered, "why are you doing this to me?"

She didn't turn around. I moved closer. I was gathering my words, thinking of the blue index card, when the idea of limited fame came into my head. I stopped. How did human beings understand each other across huge spaces except with the lowest of ideas? I have never understood what it is about rain that smells, but as I stood there behind the woman I suddenly realized I was smelling the inside of clouds. What was between us at that moment was an idea we had created ourselves. When she left with a carton of milk in her hand I couldn't speak.

On the roof that evening I looked into the sky, out over the plains, along the uneven horizon. I thought of the view my father had seen when he was a young man. I wondered whether he had imagined Star Food then. The sun was setting. The blues and oranges were mixing into black, and in the distance windows were lighting up along the hillsides.

"Tell me what I want," I said then. I moved closer to the edge of the eaves and repeated it. I looked down over the alley, into the kitchens across the way, into living rooms, bedrooms, across slate rooftops. "Tell me what I want," I called. Cars pulled in and out of the parking lot. Big rigs rushed by on the interstate. The air around me was as cool as water, the lighted swimming pools like pieces of the daytime sky. An important moment seemed to be rushing up. "Tell me what I want," I said again.

Then I heard my father open the window and come out onto the roof. He walked down and stood next to me, the bald spot on top of his head reflecting the streetlight. He took out a cigarette, smoked it for a while, pinched off the end. A bird fluttered around the light pole across the street. A car crossed below us with the words JUST MARRIED on the roof.

"Look," he said, "your mother's tried to make me understand this." He paused to put the unsmoked butt back in the pack. "And maybe I can. You think the gal's a little down and out; you don't want to kick her when she's down. Okay, I can understand that. So I've decided something, and you want to know what?"

He shifted his hands in his pockets and took a few steps toward the edge of the roof.

"You want to know what?"

"What?"

"I'm taking you off the hook. Your mother says you've got a few thoughts, that maybe you're on the verge of something, so I decided it's okay if you let the lady go if she comes in again."

"What?"

"I said it's okay if you let the gal go. You don't have to chase her."

"You're going to let her steal?"

"No," he said. "I hired a guard."

He was there the next morning in clothes that were all dark blue. Pants, shirt, cap, socks. He was only two or three years older than I was. My father introduced him to me as Mr. Sellers. "Mr. Sellers," he said, "this is Dade." He had a badge on his chest and a ring of keys the size of a doughnut on his belt. At the door he sat jingling them.

I didn't say much to him, and when I did my father came out from the back and counted register receipts or stocked impulse items near where he sat. We weren't saying anything important, though. Mr. Sellers didn't carry a gun, only the doughnut-size key ring, so I asked him if he wished he did.

"Sure," he said.

"Would you use it?"

"If I had to."

I thought of him using his gun if he had to. His hands were thick and their backs were covered with hair. This seemed to go along with shooting somebody if he had to. My hands were thin and white and the hair on them was like the hair on a girl's cheek.

During the days he stayed by the front. He smiled at customers and held the door for them, and my father brought him sodas every hour or so. Whenever the guard smiled at a customer I thought of him trying to decide whether he was looking at the shoplifter.

And then one evening everything changed.

I was on the roof. The sun was low, throwing slanted light. From beyond the New Jerusalem and behind the hills, four air force jets appeared. They disappeared, then appeared again, silver dots trailing white tails. They climbed and cut and looped back, showing dark and light like a school of fish. When they turned against the sun their wings flashed. Between the hills and the river they dipped low onto the plain, then shot upward and toward me. One dipped, the others followed. Across the New Jerusalem they turned back and made two great circles, one inside the other, then dipped again and leveled off in my direction. The sky seemed small enough for them to fall through. I could see the double tails, then the wings and the jets. From across the river they shot straight toward the store, angling up so I could see the V-wings and camouflage and rounded bomb bays, and I covered my ears, and in a moment they were across the water and then they were above me, and as they passed over they barrel-rolled and flew upside down and showed me their black cockpit glass so that my heart came up into my mouth.

I stood there while they turned again behind me and lifted back toward the hills, trailing threads of vapor, and by the time their booms subsided I knew I wanted the woman to be caught. I had seen a sign. Suddenly the sky was water-clear. Distances moved in, houses stood out against the hills, and it seemed to me that I had turned a corner and now looked over a rain-washed street. The woman was a thief. This was a simple fact and it presented itself to me simply. I felt the world dictating its course.

I went downstairs and told my father I was ready to catch her. He looked at me, rolled the chewing gum in his cheek. "I'll be damned."

"My life is making sense," I said.

When I unloaded potato chips that night I laid the bags in the aluminum racks as if I were putting children to sleep in their beds. Dust had gathered under the lip of the vegetable bins, so I swept and mopped there and ran a wet cloth over the stalls. My father slapped me on the back a couple of times. In school once I had looked through a microscope at the tip of my own finger, and now as I looked around the store everything seemed to have been magnified in the same way. I saw cracks in the linoleum floor, speckles of color in the walls.

This kept up for a couple of days, and all the time I waited for the woman to come in. After a while it was more than just waiting; I looked forward to the day when she would return. In my eyes she would find nothing but resolve. How bright the store seemed to me then when I swept, how velvety the skins of the melons beneath the sprayer bottle. When I went up to the roof I scrubbed the star with the wet cloth and came back down. I didn't stare into the clouds and I didn't think about the woman except with the thought of catching her. I described her perfectly for the guard. Her gray eyes. Her plaid dress.

After I started working like this my mother began to go to the back room in the afternoons and listen to music. When I swept the rear I heard the melodies of operas. They came from behind the stockroom door while I waited for the woman to return, and when my mother came out she had a look about her of disappointment. Her skin was pale and smooth, as if the blood had run to deeper parts.

"Dade," she said one afternoon as I stacked tomatoes in a pyramid, "it's easy to lose your dreams."

"I'm just stacking tomatoes."

She went back to the register. I went back to stacking, and my father, who'd been patting me on the back, winking at me from behind the butcher counter, came over and helped me.

"I notice your mother's been talking to you."

"A little."

We finished the tomatoes and moved on to the lettuce.

"Look," he said, "it's better to do what you have to do, so I wouldn't spend your time worrying frontwards and backwards about everything. Your life's not so long as you think it's going to be."

We stood there rolling heads of butterball lettuce up the shallow incline of the display cart. Next to me he smelled like Aqua Velva.

"The lettuce is looking good," I said.

Then I went up to the front of the store. "I'm not sure what my dreams are," I said to my mother. "And I'm never going to discover anything. All I've ever done on the roof is look at the clouds."

Then the door opened and the woman came in. I was standing in front of the counter, hands in my pockets, my mother's eyes watering over, the guard looking out the window at a couple of girls, everything revolving around the point of calm that, in retrospect, precedes surprises. I'd been waiting for her for a week, and now she came in. I realized I never expected her. She stood looking at me, and for a few moments I looked back. Then she realized what I was up to. She turned around to leave, and when her back was to me I stepped over and grabbed her.

I've never liked fishing much, even though I used to go with my father, because the moment a fish jumps on my line a tree's length away in the water I feel as if I've suddenly lost something. I'm always disappointed and sad, but now as I held the woman beneath the shoulder I felt none of this disappointment. I felt strong and good. She was thin, and I could make out the bones and tendons in her arm. As I led her back toward the stockroom, through the bread aisle, then the potato chips that were puffed and stacked like a row of pillows, I heard my mother begin to weep behind the register. Then my father came up behind me. I didn't turn around, but I knew he was there and I knew the deliberately calm way he was walking. "I'll be back as soon as I dust the melons," he said.

I held the woman tightly under her arm but despite this she moved in a light way, and suddenly, as we paused before the stockroom door, I felt as if I were leading her onto the dance floor. This flushed me with remorse. Don't spend your whole life looking backwards and forwards, I said to myself. Know what you want. I pushed the door open and we went in. The room was dark. It smelled of my whole life. I turned on the light and sat her down in the straight-back chair, then crossed the room and stood against the door. I had spoken to many children as they sat in this chair. I had frightened them, collected the candy they had tried to hide between the cushions, presented it to my father when he came in. Now I looked at the blue card. DO YOU KNOW WHAT YOU HAVE DONE? it said. DO YOU KNOW WHAT IT IS TO STEAL? I tried to think of what to say to the woman. She sat trembling slightly. I approached the chair and stood in front of her. She looked up at me. Her hair was gray around the roots.

"Do you want to go out the back?" I said.

She stood up and I took the key from under the silver samovar. My father would be there in a moment, so after I let her out I took my coat from the hook and followed. The evening was misty. She crossed the lot, and I hurried and came up next to her. We walked fast and stayed behind cars, and when we had gone a distance I turned and looked back. The stockroom door was closed. On the roof the star cast a pale light that whitened the aluminum-sided eaves.

It seemed we would be capable of a great communication now, but as we walked I realized I didn't know what to say to her. We went down the street without talking. The traffic was light, evening was approaching, and as we passed below some trees the streetlights suddenly came on. This moment has always amazed me. I knew the woman had seen it too, but it is always a disappointment to mention a thing like this. The streets and buildings took on their night shapes.

Still we didn't say anything to each other. We kept walking beneath the pale violet of the lamps, and after a few more blocks I just stopped at one corner. She went on, crossed the street, and I lost sight of her.

I stood there until the world had rotated fully into the night, and for a while I tried to make myself aware of the spinning of the earth. Then I walked back toward the store. When they slept that night, my mother would dream of discovery and my father would dream of low-grade crooks. When I thought of this and the woman I was sad. It seemed you could never really know another person. I felt alone in the world, in the way that makes me aware of sound and temperature, as if I had just left a movie theater and stepped into an alley where a light rain was falling, and the wind was cool, and, from somewhere, other people's voices could be heard.

About the Author

Ethan Canin's short stories have appeared in *The Atlantic, Esquire, Ploughshares, Chicago,* and other magazines, and have been selected for several anthologies, including *The Best American Short Stories 1985* and *1986*. In addition to the Houghton Mifflin Literary Fellowship, Canin has won a James Michener Award, an Iowa Teaching/Writing Fellowship, an Ingram Merrill Fellowship, and the Henfield/*Transatlantic Review* Award. He is twenty-seven years old and lives in Boston, Massachusetts, where he is in his last year of medical school. *Emperor of the Air* is his first book.